I0726064

A
DARK
MOST
FAIR

This is for all the sad ones; the overlooked, the struggling.
You are seen… feel your worth

First Print Edition 2025
Published in the United States by Burnt Leaf Press, LLC.

Print ISBN: 978-1-914152-22-1
eBook ISBN: 978-1-914152-23-8

www.lmriviere.com

Burnt Leaf Press is an independent publisher of serialized, digital, and printed fiction, run by authors and designers, for authors and designers.
Visit www.burntleafpress.com to discover our full library of content.

NO generative AI was used (or needed) to draft, revise, edit, design, or lay out this work, to the knowledge of the author or the publisher--- nor do we condone its use.

Developmental edits by KM_West Creative
Copyedits by Ramona Mihai

Cover art:
Bethan Lientie- lientie.co.uk
@artis.marginalia

Interior art:
Anita Zaramella- inner leaf (anitazaramella.wordpress.com)
Marta Riva- title page, chapter breaks (intotheforest-illustrations)
Brady Moller- inner layout and formatting

Content Warning

A
DARK
MOST
FAIR
LM RIVIERE

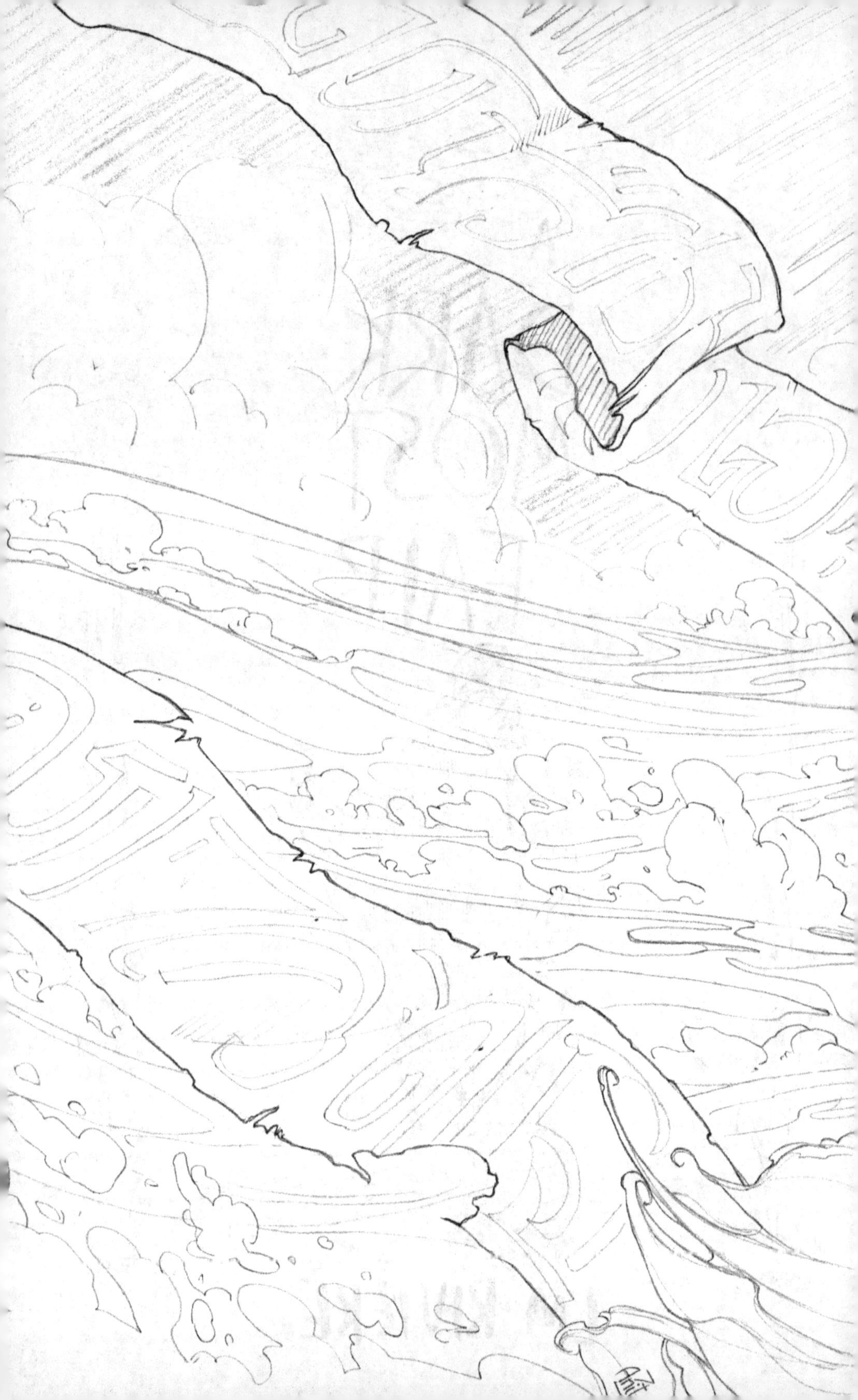

The Others Are Not To Be Trusted

You should know, I did it.

Before you trouble yourself to read any further, you won't find an innocent woman in these pages.

I am every bit as evil as they say I am.

A murderer.

A liar.

A kinslayer.

The gods, they say, save their worst punishments for those like me. Those who covet what isn't theirs.

Those who slay their own blood.

Those who lie about it after.

I'm a woman who murdered for a man. There isn't a hell black enough for one such as me.

I'm every inch a sinner.

And I will get what I deserve.

Soon.

One

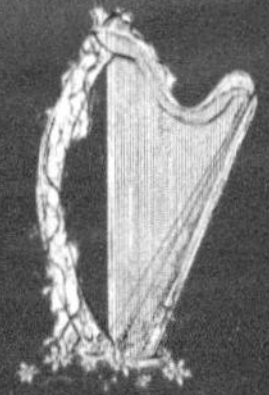

I wasn't always a villain.

I used to be a perfectly normal, happy little girl. I played with poppets, chased butterflies, and made as much mischief as possible. I snuck apple tarts from the kitchens every autumn, was allergic to shoes and veils, and my braids were always dirty from sleeping on the flagstones in my father's library—my little knees curled up, my mother's cat purring at my nape. I played hide-and-chase with Cook's children in the mud outside, sneaking in apples from the orchard, or the odd shiny pebble for Cook's ever-growing collection.

My mother despaired of me, but bought me a wooden sword every market day, nonetheless.

I had such dreams then.

I wanted to be a dragon, a fairy, or a hero from the old tales. I'd listen hard to every yarn my mother told, hardened honey smearing both cheeks, a fire in my heart. I would be a noble sorcerer, a clockmaker, or a witch. I would run away and live in the woods. I would become queen of the gnomes and mushrooms. I would steal away to live with the Dagda in Tír na nÓg, and learn to play the harp at Aengus Mac Óg's knee. I might even cast my lot in with the Danish hordes, become a fierce raider, endlessly plundering at sea.

My mother would gaze upon me and smile. Her Dierdre, her princess. So small and sweet, foolish and fierce.

I was just seven summers old when my mother died.

She took her tales with her.

Soon enough, my father wed again.

The woman who replaced my mother didn't care for apple tarts, my father's library, or the fanciful dreams of a motherless child. Hester, my father's new wife, vowed to make a lady of me so I might never shame her at meals. It was then I learnt of the word 'dowry,' and how it would come to dominate my life. According to

Hester, a king's daughter has but one duty, one reason to exist: her bride price.

A princess exists to be sold.

My 'dowry' became my world.

From beneath her stark white lashes, Hester saw to everything.

My poppets were burned. I was forbidden apple tarts or sweets in general, for fear I'd grow as plump as my mother had been. My chamber would be locked at night so I would no longer seek the warmth of my father's library. Muddy toes were replaced with dancing shoes. Hide-and-chase supplanted with needlepoint and darning. My braids were collected into an uncomfortable knot at my nape every morning, and if a single strand wiggled out of place by supper, I would be sent to bed without a bite. The tales I so loved were replaced with new stories: the Penitent Maid, the Obedient Daughter, and the Good Wife. Dragons and gnomes were banished forever.

Years passed, and I grew tame where once I'd been wild.

Then, Calanthe came.

I soon learned that unwanted attention might be better than none.

My sister was born four winters after Hester took my mother's place. The moment her cries pierced the halls, I was forgotten. One moment I was poked and prodded from dawn to dusk, straightened, lengthened— corrected. No books, no games, no laughter. Only folding, knitting, needlework, and plaiting. Scrubbed cheeks replaced tart-smeared lips. Tight, uncomfortably coiffed tresses replaced dirty braids.

Duty replaced curiosity.

Day and night, I was hounded, a torn tapestry that needed constant mending.

And then nothing.

The moment Calanthe's wails echoed throughout the keep for the first time, I faded into the stonework. My father's golden wife had given him the perfect, golden daughter. Their happiness was acute and wholly private. They took meals in Hester's apartments in the South tower. My father skipped court more than thrice weekly. He met with courtiers in his library so he might be close to hand if Hester needed him.

After a while, Hester sat at his elbow, holding their golden daughter at her breast. Her soft voice and radiant beauty captivated every audience. The king glowed with pride for his handsome, elegant family. By the time Calanthe was old enough to sit at their feet and play with her dolls, visiting dignitaries fell all over themselves to offer her this or that prince or lordling's hand.

Meanwhile, I was nowhere to be seen.

My father preferred I remain out of sight.

Hester stopped having her women visit my rooms.

A princess in her castle, and yet I was so nearly invisible that even Cook's kitchen hands or the warriors and squires training in the fields stared through. Whatever hopes they once held for me at seven summers had vanished, replaced by frowns, puzzled glances, clipped words, and outright neglect. It seemed my father and his new family no longer had need of my bride-price. No expectation that it would fetch anywhere near what Calanthe's could. After all, at barely 10 summers old, she was already the talk of the kingdom— the radiant daughter of the King of Ulaid. Any prince would count himself lucky to win such a lovely wife. And what's worse, Calanthe had perfect manners, too.

Her voice was sweet where mine was low.

Her eyes were bright where mine were dark.

Her steps were light where mine were heavy.

Calanthe preferred songs and laughter to the hush and quiet of the old tales. She loved to sing and dance, smile and make merry. Her needlepoint, even as a child, was so fine the women would praise her to the heavens each day. Her braids never needed replaiting, her feet were always properly covered, her face never smeared with jam.

Where was I, you ask?

In my rooms, in my father's library, or walking the hills with just one maid for a guard. I wasn't winsome enough for a knight, you see. What man would trouble himself to carry off such a dull, plain, unaccomplished princess as I? What man would want a wife who was taller than he, who was unfashionably dark, her eyes green and wild, her bearing proud, challenging? No prince wanted a wife who could quote Ovid but couldn't darn a sock. That much was clear.

I was second-best, and no one let me forget it.

WHEN SHE WAS FIFTEEN SUMMERS OLD, MY FATHER AN-
nounced a tourney for Calanthe's name day. His councilors expected a fine turnout, as my sister's hand was,
by that point, the greatest prize in the land. Tales of
her beauty circled the courts of every great king in Eire,
even the High King at Tara. Rumors spread that my
father would only offer her hand to the bravest, most
celebrated warlord at his midsummer tourney, where
he would choose her husband from among the victors.

If you are foreign and perhaps don't know how
much my people love a competition, let me assure you,
the very challenge of the game was enough to motivate
the meanest spearmen to try his luck. There were fewer
things an Eirean *curadh* loved more than competition,
maiden prizes, or no. Messengers rode into the courtyard on a daily basis, bearing gifts, baubles, verse, or
wine— and as ever, a promise that this or that noble
lordling or cocksure knight would become my sister's
groom. Reading each nauseating love letter aloud,
Calanthe would cover her rosebud mouth and sigh.
She would moon over the bold declarations within and

titter about them with her maids. Her mother would shake her head and focus on her weaving beside the fireplace, muttering about silly games.

Hester was not consulted about Calanthe's tourney, and her resentment was plain. She tugged at her needlework with an irritated tilt of her full lower lip. "Calanthe, love. Perhaps we could do without a second reading tonight?"

Calanthe dimpled. "Yes, Mother."

But her sky-blue eyes cut to me at my place in the window seat, and I groaned aloud.

"Don't look at me, Cal," I said. "I agree with your mother."

Hester made a rude sound that I ignored.

We didn't agree often, but she made it clear that my support was never expected nor appreciated. Still, Calanthe didn't seem to mind. She always asked me for my opinion, whether I wished to share it or not.

"Why shouldn't I be pleased?" she whined for my benefit. It used to work with me when she was small, and every now and then she would attempt to trot that pony back out in hopes it might sway me to ride to her rescue.

It rarely did.

"Because every word someone else scribbled for them there is a lie, Cal."

"You don't know that!"

"No?"

"No!"

"How many of these men have actually met you?"

She chewed her full lower lip.

"Besides," I gave her a hard look, "most of these fools can't even read, let alone would bother to flatter a young girl's pride with such talk."

"We can read!" she protested.

"Aye, our father fancies himself a learned man and does not suffer fools among his household. Women included."

Hester cleared her throat.

Well, most of the women, anyway.

"You don't know that any of these lords are unlettered. You're just jealous." Calanthe sniffed disdainfully.

She was *half* right, but that hardly mattered.

"Cal, if you keep pretending to be a simple girl, our father really will marry you to one of these brutes. Where will you be then?"

She didn't answer, but Olga, one of Hester's women, raised her nose. "It seems to me that the princess should be honored to hold the admiration of so many noble lords. How horrible it would be for her to become an old maid, like *someone* else we know."

I smiled back.

I did have very straight teeth, despite my otherwise ungainly appearance.

Wolfish teeth, some whispered behind my back.

I was satisfied to watch Olga flinch.

The Norse girls among Hester's coterie were all un-lettered, uncultured cows with straw for brains. They'd arrived with Hester from Dubh-Lin after my mother had died, and had plagued me ever since. Nothing I did was good enough for any of them, and Olga herself used to pinch my cheeks till they bled whenever I dis-pleased her mistress.

Which was to say, very often.

To Hester's women, my sister need only find a man to take her into his household where she might squeeze out babies and darn socks until she eventually died a soundless, obedient death.

I disagreed.

We were noble Eirean women.

The blood of the Dagda himself.

The High King was my great-uncle.

Therefore, my sister could do a far sight better than some pimple-faced lordling who likely couldn't read. If you're confused by this point about my feelings for Calanthe, don't worry, you're not alone. I, too, could never decide if I loved or hated her… or which feeling ruled from one day to the next. All I knew for certain was that she was my little sister, and I knew she was a lot smarter than she looked. If only she would show it every once in a while.

"Olga," I said sweetly. "Don't you have chamber pots to scour?"

The older woman's mouth closed with a snap. She turned back to her needlepoint without another word.

Hester raised a brow at me, and I swallowed my triumph.

"Cal," I said, more evenly. "I am sure you will hear all manner of romantic gibberish in those pages, but use your head, not your eyes."

She let out a very put-upon sigh. "Father wants an alliance with King Mark."

"Very good. And?"

"King Ælla."

"Right."

"He wants me to be seen at this tourney."

"Why?"

"So he can bargain for my dowry later."

"Which means you'll marry who he says you'll marry, but certainly not any of the fools he's invited to compete in this ridiculous display. Who do you think would benefit Ulaid most?"

She let out a powerful breath. "Neither. He'll choose Conor of Munster."

"Very good, why?"

"For turnips."

"It's pronounced *agriculture*, Cal."

"Same difference," she droned.

I set my scroll down. "And why would he do that?"

"Because Father would never marry me to a foreign raider."

As she said this, her eyes guiltily slid to her mother.

Ælla was Hester's uncle, and although she and my father had a visibly happy marriage, he would rather die than begrudge her people a single acre in Ulaid. The Danes had settled old Dubh-Lin decades before, but that didn't mean they were wholly welcome. Nor did it mean that the rest of the Eirean kings trusted their flimsy treaty a whit. Besides, Ælla's sons were all dead save his last, a dribbling dolt named Erik, or so I'd read in one of father's reports.

I highly doubted such a man would dare to show his face here.

King Mark of Kernow, on the other hand, had many dashing warriors waiting for a chance to peacock before an Eirean lord.

My sister's presence would just make it more sporting.

Hester glared up at me. "Must you encourage this kind of talk? It is unwomanly."

"No, Mother," Calanthe broke in. "Deirdre's right. I should stop being silly."

"What Deirdre does not say," Hester's voice raised slightly, her attention still on the needlepoint in her lap, "is that your father will grant you the right to choose your mate, if he is worthy."

I snorted.

But Hester pressed on. "The reason she won't say so is because by rights, such a choice would have been hers, had her mother lived. But, alas, the old lady is dead, and I now sit at her father's side."

I went very still.

"Only the daughter of a queen may choose her suitor from among a worthy few."

"My mother was queen," I said softly.

"No, she wasn't, child. She was a poor landsman's daughter who your father raised above her station. That lack of birthright stains you. A pity you didn't inherit her beauty."

Heat raced into my cheeks.

"Take it back."

"I cannot take back the truth, my dear."

I stood up, hands shaking. "My mother was of noble Eirean blood. My father named her queen when they wed."

"The second son of a powerless clansman is hardly a nobleman."

"Take it *back*!"

"I will not. The clans no longer hold power in Eire, girl. Your father hasn't held a tourney for you nor bothered to seek suitors for your hand because frankly, no one wants you. I am sad to say, there is no benefit in offering your hand. Certainly not in Ulaid."

"*Mother*!" Calanthe hissed.

"Were you at least the smallest bit beautiful, I could barter your dowry for one of my uncle's *foreign* vassals, but why bother? None would have you. You're too tall, your eyes spark greed, and you speak when you should keep your mouth shut."

Olga covered her face over a giggle, and Hester's other nameless cows chimed in.

Calanthe didn't share their mirth.

She went bright as an apple, and reached for my hand.

I would have none of her pity.

I flung her hand aside and ran from the room, utterly humiliated.

Two

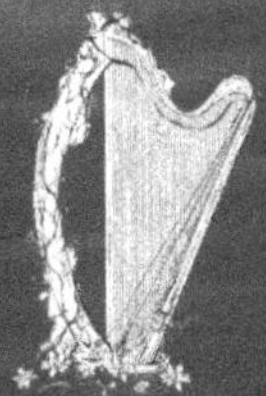

Everyone needs a place to hide.

For me, it was my father's library. None of Hester's women would dare chase me in here even if they had an interest. I hid among the stacks in the dark, weeping into my hem and wishing I were dead. Everything Hester had said was true. Just because my mother had been queen for a time did not mean I would ever be one.

Her family was ancient and powerful, once.

No longer.

When my father met my mother, they'd been of minor consequence for some generations. Apparently, my mother's great-grandfather had challenged my father's grandfather for the right to rule these Uí Néill lands. Needless to say, he lost, and his family's fortunes never improved. My mother did have a noble name, as I'd said so proudly.

Once.

That name no longer held any power, and many of my father's councilors had considered her not much higher in status than a concubine. If she had lived to bear my father a son, that would have changed her stars and mine. But that hadn't happened. And here I was over fifteen years later, alone, friendless, and unloved by my own family.

I had no one to complain to. And no one to blame.

Hester was everything my mother hadn't been, which was no doubt why my father's landsmen worked so hard to push the match forward. Her uncle was a great king despite the fact that he was a Dane. Ælla held lands in every isle from here to Daneland and even some as far away as mighty Francia and the snow-swept tundras of Rus. He was paid *weregild* by more men than even our own High King, and could summon more warriors than my own father and the High King put together.

Ælla was a force to be reckoned with. A king of kings.

My mother's family owned a small holding and six dozen head of sheep.

So you see, my sister and I were unequal.

And there was nothing I could do about it.

I wanted to be seen, same as Calanthe.

I wanted suitors, same as Calanthe.

I wanted to be admired, same as Calanthe.

But I wasn't beautiful.

I wasn't ladylike.

And I had the wrong mother.

The thought made me weep the harder for the memory of my mother's warm eyes. While everything I had said to my sister was true, what Hester said was equally true.

I *was* jealous of Calanthe.

I had always been.

The moment she was born, I became a ghost. An inconvenient leftover.

Once, when I was younger, I had tipped myself from the North Gate, in hopes that I would meet my mother in the Otherworld or simply sink into the soil to join

The Others at their games. Instead, I'd broken my arm and spent nine weeks in my room wound in itchy white linen. My father stopped visiting me then. Stopped asking for me soon after.

I would ask myself '*why*.'

Why couldn't I disappear?

Why wasn't I brave enough to throw myself into the sea?

Just as I began to sink into this familiar pool of self-pity, I heard something.

The room was every bit as cold as it always was, being that each of the windows held only wooden slats, and the summer sun did little to keep the cutting Ulaid wind out. The room was gloomy, too, given the oil lamps my father preferred could only be lit at full dark. Vellum was precious and delicate, after all, thus torches and candles were forbidden without good cause.

The space was quiet as usual, with only the noise from the yard filtering through the shutters.

I held my breath.

What if my father found me here again? I wasn't allowed to be in here without my father or his librarian. That hardly stopped me, most days. What prisoner would ignore the opportunity to temporarily escape into worlds they'd never glimse with their own eyes? Still, I didn't long to be discovered disobeying him again. This time, he might actually beat me, as Hester vowed he would.

What if he locked me in my room again? Worse, what if he took my allotted scrolls away altogether?

The sound came again, something like a muffled bell or the barest hint of a sigh.

I raised my eyes to a cobwebbed shelf just below the timber ceiling.

There was nothing there. Just musty scrolls and a few long-forgotten sheepskins that might one day become scrolls, if anyone remembered where they were. There wasn't enough light to see how many items were stacked up there.

The chime came again.

This time, it felt like a voice.

Someone calling for help.

I shot to my feet.

My mother warned me about hearing bells in the dark.

Everyone's mother had warned them about hearing bells *anywhere* they shouldn't. I backed away so fast, I knocked into the shelf behind me. To my horror, it wobbled, and then suddenly teetered forward, knocking me into the very casing I'd been trying to escape. In a flurry of cracking wood, flying dust, falling sheepskin, and tumbling scrolls, I hit the stone floor— hard. Coughing, I quickly struggled up to my knees, waving at the air in front of my face until the dust cleared.

Blood drained from my cheeks as I looked around.

The library was a mess. Several of my father's most precious scrolls were scattered across the rushes, some of them torn. Beyond that, the shelves before and behind me toward the heavy oak door were splintered or collapsed altogether. Dust and crumbling vellum coated the floor like a thick woolen shroud.

I heard the bell sigh on the floor beside my bleeding hand and recoiled.

This scroll was old, perhaps older than any I'd ever seen before. The skin was a vellum so dark, it might have been tanned. At either end perched a bronze cap, and a torn bit of faded red linen braided across its middle. From that, at the end of a brittle leather cord, was tied an iron bell. It appeared harmless enough now. Its scroll lay harmlessly in the rushes beneath the surviving end of its shelf with so many others.

Now, the bell lay silent.

Slowly, painfully, I pushed myself to my feet. I'd cut my fingers on a split wooden beam. Several long splinters rent the flesh of my palm, making me cry out. One was nearly the length of my index finger. Tearing up, I jerked the offensive object out of my weeping skin, blood now running freely down my arm. I tucked it under my belt, hoping to staunch the bleeding some until I could make it downstairs to Cook. She could mend it for me. Although, my father would surely murder me soon after.

I turned to limp through the door, when I heard the sound again. The little bell chimed so loud, I thought the whole keep would hear it. An angry protest. My head whipped back around. There, on the floor, was the braided scroll with the bell.

It hadn't moved an inch.

I stared for several heartbeats, nearly daring it to sound again and prove me fully mad.

It didn't.

It lay there in the ruin of my father's library, a broken scroll tied with a harmless bell.

An overwhelming urge overcame me then.

A power like a lake at full flood compelled me back to the floor.

I reached out with my bloodied hand.

The bell was silent as I raced from the room with it tucked under my arm.

MY FATHER WAS FURIOUS, OF COURSE.

The scrolls in that library would fetch more silver than all the gems in my stepmother's bower.

He found me in my room after Cook had finished torturing me. I'd broken two fingers, and she made quite a lot of noise about what evils wood could unleash within human flesh, tutting over the sight of my filthy dress and scraped knee. She smothered my open wound in a mixture of raw honey and nettle before wrapping my fingers up tight enough to keep me from bending them.

Naturally, she had no choice but to tell my father what had happened. I didn't begrudge her. *She* didn't destroy the library because she felt sorry for herself. I did. So, I would face my punishment with all the grace I could muster.

What else could I do?

Not long after I hobbled up the last step to my room and opened the door, my father came stomping up the stairs. The whole of the keep, being built of strong oak and pine, surely must have felt that dreadful march.

"Deirdre," he said, evenly. He didn't bellow or rage; that was not my father's way. But that hardly masked the black fire in his eyes. He was dark, like me, and had the same hawkish nose and tall frame. "I should have you beaten."

"Yes," I agreed, resigned.

I couldn't feign innocence with my hand dressed in more linen than my skirt.

He stepped into the room and closed the door behind him. "I hear you've been disrespectful to your mother."

"She is *not* my mother."

He seemed to soften then, just a bit. "No, more's the pity, but you will respect her or lose the blessings of my hall."

I wanted to argue with him, but what would be the point? He would blame me no matter what I said.

"Yes, Father," I lied.

He watched me silently for a few moments.

I tried not to squirm under his eye.

"Your bitterness and pride will be your undoing one day, Deirdre."

"*My* pride?"

"I can understand why you bear no love for Hester, as you feel she replaced your mother."

"She, quite literally, has."

"But what of Calanthe? Your sister loves you even if you do not appreciate her."

I looked away, my throat burning with unshed tears.

"Was my mother truly queen, Father?"

He paused, taking a seat in my window box. "Is that what this is about?"

"Was she queen, or… or…?"

"My *leman*?"

All the heat in my body rushed to my eyebrows. "Y-yes."

"Had she lived, or bore me a son, your lot would be different, yes."

"Hester's family has more coin. Is that really all?"

"More or less."

How unfair life was.

"So, I am to suffer every indignity simply because my grandfather wasn't rich enough to warrant a bloody contest for my hand."

"Deirdre, it's more complex than that."

"What am I missing? My younger sister is the 'fairest' maid in all Ulaid. I am merely an afterthought."

"Your younger sister is celebrated far and wide because she is the grand-niece of King Ælla of Daneland, and the daughter of the Uí Néill of Ulaid. She is a strong lure for powerful purses, and I must play the hand I am given."

"And me?"

He sighed long and hard. "I wish it could be otherwise, Deirdre, but yes, in this contest, you must be second."

That was it then.

I was born to be unhappy.

An accident of birth.

A barely coiled anger slithered between my ribs.

"And what of my happiness, Father? Shall I have nothing, be nothing, take nothing? Am I to flit here and there as a shadow, never seen, never heard, just a sad ghost with bad luck?"

I could see the hurt I'd caused him and didn't care.

He was like me.

Once wounded, he'd rise to the occasion.

Storms crossed his brow.

"What do you want from me, Daughter?"

"I wish to choose."

"Choose what?"

"Who shall take me from this place and make me his lady."

He stood. "Do you think to command me?"

"No. I will accept second-place after my undeserving sister in exchange for the right to choose my own husband."

"I will not—"

"Father," I argued, summoning every ounce of my courage. "I want to be gone as much as Hester wishes me to leave. Let me choose a man and quit this place for good."

"You are a princess."

"According to you and Hester, I'm a low-level lady at best and will not be missed."

"You are my daughter!"

"One you barely speak to, barely see, and hardly ever look for."

"You will not scold *me*," he growled, stalking forward. "You will obey. That is all."

He didn't give me a chance to rebut that statement.

He ripped my door open and exited, pausing only to turn and point a finger at me.

"Bitterness and pride!"

When the door slammed shut hard enough to rattle its casings, I threw myself against my quilt and cried until dry racking sobs took over. I was a prisoner, locked in a family that despised me, who longed to be rid of me, yet would not let me go.

Unbidden, I thought again of the sea, imagining the way the waves might curl white and clean against the rocks below the cliff. What if I asked to be sent away? To live as a widow or spinster in a small cottage, alone? Would that be such a bad fate? I squeezed my eyes shut, as if that would strangle the thought dead. Thinking of such things only made me feel worse, further eroding what remained of my self worth.

Then, I heard it.

The hollow toll of a tiny bronze bell. So close to my ear, I jumped.

The bell sounded once more while I gawped at it… even though it hadn't moved an inch from its hiding place half-stuffed beneath my pillow. I scrambled back- ward, hand flying to the space above my heart.

The bell chimed mournfully, as if I'd somehow wounded it by running away.

Not knowing what else to do or if I was indeed going mad, I opened my mouth to ask:

"What do you want?"

The bell rattled a muffled response.

My pulse in my nose, I wrung my hands.

I regularly took my meals with the maids in the kitchen, where I was safely out of Hester's line of sight. Cook filled that time regaling everyone with tales of The Others— the doom-givers. The Others, she would say, brought misfortune to mortals without fail. Their touch spread madness and fear, mystification, and os- tracization. To be 'fey touched' was no blessing.

It was a curse.

Every Eirean knew the cunning folk had spent eons trapped in the Otherworld, forever seething over the mortal theft of their ancestral lands during the age of heroes. Naturally, the Old Gods would look for any opportunity to bedevil us. Being haunted by a ringing bell that did not move was a bad sign.

The bell rang more insistently.

Well aware of what would happen if I raced downstairs to ask Cook how to handle a spectral bell, I took a deep breath and did the next best thing. I grabbed the offensive scroll and launched to my feet, opened my shutters, and hurled it into the night.

Three

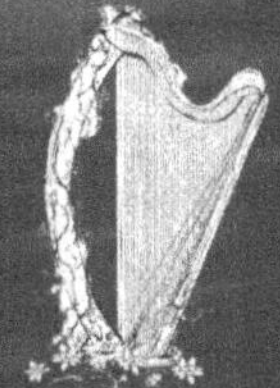

At breakfast the next day, I learned the full scope of my father's ire. I wasn't merely to be ignored as I had thought. No, the indignity was to be much keener than that. I knew something was wrong the moment I stepped into the kitchen to receive my breakfast. The staff sniggered behind their hands within my line of sight, or eyed me from the edges of the room, whispering to each other. I had expected some tongue-wagging after nearly destroying the library and the subsequent upbraiding my father had so publicly given me last night. But in my gut, I felt a cold splash of fear that I was missing something. Maybe it was the hushed invocation of my stepmother's name that brought my fears to the fore, or maybe I was merely hyper-senstitive to gossip in the first place? Whichever were most true, my skin blistered under the undeclared 'something' I was not yet privy to.

Cook confirmed it with her eyes long before I opened my mouth to ask what was going on.

"My poor lass," she moaned under her breath. Cook was probably the only person in the keep that genuinely cared about my feelings. She pulled me closer. "Don't you pay attention to any of these silly creatures?"

I groaned. "The library?"

"Worse."

My brows came up. "My father?"

"Worse."

Brida, I thought.

What's worse than a whole castle full of people listening to your father tell you how bitter and proud you are?

Then she told me.

I was to be my sister's lady-in-waiting while the warriors and noblemen of the realm came to compete for her hand.

Not only was I, the eldest daughter of the King of Ulaid, to have my place usurped by a girl barely out of swaddling, I was to endure it while holding her hem and passing notes from her would-be suitors. My father couldn't have scored a deeper wound if he'd plunged a knife in my belly. The humiliation was total.

I sank into the nearest seat rather than slip to the flagstones in shock. Cook fidgeted as she was wont to do when she had no idea how to manage me.

"Now, it's not all bad, love. Everyone knows these contests only bring out the second-sons and lesser lordlings. They're the ones with aught to prove, right enough. Course, they'll sing your sister's praises to their fathers and maybe you'll be rid of her soon. Her and her whey-faced barbarian mother." She screwed her nose up.

Cook was also the only other person in the keep that hated my stepmother as much as I did, too.

I bit my lip.

What was I going to do?

If I denied my father's wishes, he really could banish me to the north with the unwed mothers and other misbehaving womenfolk. If I did as he asked, I would be degrading myself before every lord and warrior from here to Dubh-Lin.

By rights, the eldest daughter should be wed a full season in advance of the younger even being announced in a public capacity. If my mother had lived, or I'd had an elder brother to inherit my father's title as the Uí Néill, I would have had a dowry worthy of the firstborn daughter of the King of Ulaid. I would have received the letters, the gifts, and all the other trappings Calanthe now enjoyed as the prospective daughter-in-law of a great lord— perhaps even the son of the High King himself— even if that might be its own sort of punishment. The heir apparent was not likely to follow his father to the throne. But that was beside the point.

Unfortunately, Hester's uncle outranked my father.

Which meant, Calanthe outranked me… *publicly*.

More than that. The length and breadth of the Isle would now know how truly worthless I was to my father.

My cheeks burst into flames.

My eyes swelled with water.

Cook jerked me out of my seat, steering me into the vestibule.

"I know it don't make much nevermind to a man such as your father, but your mother was the only queen any of us have a care for. You don't let this darken your brow, love. You're a princess. A proper Eirean lady. Don't give your stepmam the pleasure of your tears."

I nodded, wiping my nose on my apron.

"What should I do?"

Cook snorted. "You hold your head high and look down your nose at every bloody one of them. You wear your finest gowns, wear that luscious dark hair down your back like a silk curtain, rouge your lips, and keep a smirk in the corner of your mouth. That's what you do."

I choked back a sob rather than disgrace myself further.

People were watching.

"H-how? I have no fine gowns, no rouge."

"Never you mind. Your mother had the finest things. I'll have them in your room by tomorrow morn."

"But they're in Hester's rooms! She'll never let me have them."

She patted my hands. "You let me worry about that. You go take a bath and triple-plait your hair, like I showed you. All them black waves free and flowing will fair stop a man's heart, I'm sure."

"But—"

"No 'buts.' You must obey your father but that doesn't mean you need to lessen yourself for that whey-faced Nord's get. No disrespect to your sister, she's but a sweet child being led in all this, but that mother of hers ought to respect our customs as we're meant to respect her."

I floated in a daze while she led me back up to my room, petting me like a kicked dog. She buzzed around me for a further ten minutes, but I heard nothing she said. The moment my toe cleared the open doorway, I heard the bell; a soft, insistent peal.

My eyes snapped to my coverlet, and there, peeking out from beneath my pillow, was the very same scroll I'd tossed out of my window the night before. I didn't blink, for fear my mind had conjured the scene just to taunt me.

The bell trilled again, this time, testily, but Cook appeared to hear nothing.

I would have asked her, though I was well aware of what she would say.

She patted my hands once more and left, leaving me wide-eyed, trembling, and alone.

Staring at the thing on my bed.

The bell rattled accusingly, and I knew.

It had happened.

The thing everyone said would happen, eventually.

I'd gone mad.

I stood glaring down at the scroll for nearly an hour, trying to decide what to do.

Clearly, the bell wanted the scroll to be read.

And clearly, I was utterly, irrevocably touched in the head.

Scrolls do not have wishes any more than bells could ring by themselves. The bell made a muffled sort of jingle that one might take for a groan. I didn't know what to do. I didn't know who to ask. I didn't know if I should throw it back outside, keep quiet and still, or run screaming down the stairs to Cook's chamber. I worried at my nails while I considered my options.

Mad girls were taken north, ne'er to return.

Would that be so bad? The obnoxious voice in my head asked.

You could wed who you want… or not at all.

You could keep your own garden, wear what you wish, see who you wish. You could be your own mistress, and never answer to your stepmam again.

I snorted to myself.

I would also be exquisitely poor, forgotten, and likely starving. I didn't have much experience with the people, but what I had seen did not inspire envy. Every winter folk in rags came to Emain Macha in droves, seeking shelter, warmth, and food. Some came bearing wool from the summer sheer. Some came with berries, nuts, and herbs foraged from the lakelands. Some came with stinking salted fish, sealskins, and other goods plucked from Manannan's Sea to the east. Most came with nothing save the rags on their backs, and the sickly children they could scarce feed. My father was a good king. He tried to keep his kingdom from famine and blight. But it happened anyway.

I asked my mother once why so many outside the walls looked so hollow and thin. She told me people were like seeds carried on a breeze. The wind didn't care whether we were dropped in rich, black soil or left moldering on barren crags.

I wouldn't be spared if I shared my madness with anyone inside these walls.

So, what was I to do?

The bell was silent, as if with bated breath in anticipation of victory.

I could throw it out the window again.

Watch it drift on the wind, or bounce from the rocks below.

But I knew it would return.

I could carry it back to my father's library and bury it beneath the same dusty tomes. Somewhere secret? Somewhere even I wouldn't find it? What good was madness if it couldn't help you lose something as small and tedious as this?

But I knew the suggestion would torment me until I retrieved it.

Perhaps, I could sneak it into Calanthe's chamber and let it drive her to distraction.

The bell seemed to scoff.

I could take it to the lake and let the current carry it to the sea.

The bell fluttered in alarm.

I smiled.

That's what I would do.

Path chosen, I grabbed my mother's shawl from the chest at the end of my bed and snatched the offensive scroll from its hiding place beneath my pillow. I would roll it up, tuck it beneath my cloak, and carry it from the keep. After I'd flung it into the lake, I would return very late indeed, but facing my father's wroth for running away was far preferable to becoming a fey-touched madwoman.

I was smirking at my cleverness when something happened. My fingers closed over the scroll for mere moments, but in that span, a profound malaise crept through my heart. This crushing regret, this absolute loneliness seemed to seep into my veins and still my blood.

I gasped, letting the scroll tumble to the furs beside my bed.

The bell rattled piteously.

Such loneliness.

Even I, who had no friends and was loved by none, had never felt such a sunless morosity.

I dropped to my knees.

The bell was hushed, but I knew it was begging me to save it.

Could I refuse?

I should.

But would I?

My mother had also once told me a tale about a woman who found a lost foal in a thicket at twilight. Believing the mare must have been scared away or slain, the woman brought the foal home and nursed it. In a half year's time, the foal became tall, broad, and black as the spaces between the stars; its red eyes patient and knowing. One day, the woman came to feed the foal what barley she had to spare from her winter stores. When she opened the foal's stall, the foal declared that he'd had enough barley and preferred meat.

The woman answered that she had none, and hoped this might suffice. But it would not. The beast changed its shape. A pooka stood before her, amorphous and black as ink. Before it gobbled her up, it thanked her for her kindness with a garish leer.

So, you see, pity was not always the bargain one hoped for.

Then again… surely, whatever the bell contained, was alive.

Whatever was concealed within this scroll, it bore feelings, memories, sadness. Couldn't I empathize? Didn't I understand such loneliness? Besides, what if it had been put there against its will? Could I condemn another?

Conflicted, I decided to address the source directly.

"Are you ever going to leave?"

Its lack of response suggested this was unlikely.

"I could burn you."

I had an impression it gasped.

I *should* burn the offensive object.

Every instinct told me this would be the wisest course.

But, what would I do when it did not burn? When it reappeared under my pillow, unharmed?

If it could travel around the keep on its own, did that also mean it couldn't be destroyed? I had no idea how magic even worked, let alone whatever flavor of magic this thing possessed. I was no sage or wise woman. I was just a girl who lived in a cold, unhappy home. What did I know about anything? The dust motes floating between me and the shutters held no answer. The blackened stones of my hearth were equally unhelpful. Nervous fingers in my mouth again, I tasted blood from a much worn nail bed.

The bell tolled mournfully evoking forlorn images of loss and pain in my mind.

It wanted me to know it felt its situation, keenly.

And I believed it.

Danu, help me.

My resolve slipped away.

This scroll had chosen its victim well, I mused.

I could not throw it into the fire.

"If I do as you wish," I said, finally. "You will leave me and mine in peace. That is fair."

The bell chimed eagerly.

"If you harm me, I will curse you with my last breath."

The bell trilled agreeably.

This was a terrible idea.

I knew it. I *felt* it. The Others were not to be trusted.

Whatever this scroll held would break its word. It wouldn't be able to help itself.

The old tales spoke of miseries out of measure.

I'd never heard another kind.

The bell rattled irritably, as if to ask what I could know about such things. Frightened but improbably moved to pity, I reached out and untied its leather binding. The bell tinkled its last, as if in incomprehensible relief.

The room shivered around me.

A shimmer of light.

A deafening pop.

A wheezing cry.

And then, a mannish shape stepped from the open scroll in a brief wash of pale color. It sucked in a hard lungful of air and immediately collapsed like a broken sail.

I scrambled backward.

My eyes wide as supper plates, I covered my mouth to hide a scream.

The figure bore the shape of a man, though it was far too thin and small to be reasonably compared. The creature was not much larger than a child, really, although twisted and gnarled at the joints, like an old man. Its skin gray and mottled, a sickly, fish-belly shade that spoke of eons out of the sun and air. Long, stringy hair like cobwebs dangled from its patchy scalp. What clothing it wore, sloughed from its tiny, knobby frame like ribbons. It cracked open an eye so green, I thought of lake grass in the springtime.

Bony, blackened fingers reached out to me.

"Mistress," its dusty, too-high voice called. "I t-thank you."

Before I could utter a word in return, the creature shuddered, then dropped in a dead faint, leaving me to stare down at him in silent, incredulous terror.

What had I done?

What doom had I invited into my life?

Four

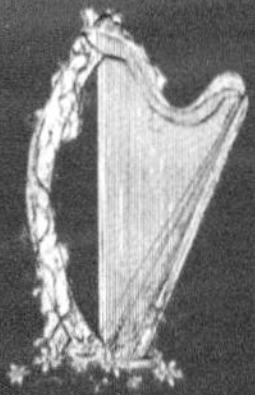

After hours of watching my charge sleep, I settled on a course of action. I covered him with my mother's quilt and pushed the furs he slept on beneath my bed. He was so small, the chore wasn't too difficult. He didn't seem to notice anything I did, just curled in on himself in his sleep, plainly exhausted. There wasn't much I could do now except make sure no one came up here and discovered him.

I didn't need to feign discomfiture.

I could tell without looking into the polished bronze mirror on my larder that all the blood had long since quit my face. My eyes must have gone blue around the rim, and my lips grown pale as thistledown. My hair, not having seen a comb in two days, was a wild, tangled thicket of greasy curls. My dress was rumpled and unwashed, the stays at my throat undone and my faded sleeves untidy.

I'm sure I looked a fright.

Thankfully, this is exactly what I needed at the moment.

Once Cook saw me come again into the kitchen, she threw down her ladle and immediately set to fussing.

She plied me with broth, nettle tea, and then promptly sent back up to bed with the promise to keep everyone well away. My alarming state would be circulated around the keep in a trice, therefore, no one would expect me at supper. Before she took her leave, Cook promised to bring more broth and bread later that evening. This was the first time I was glad not to be as coddled as my sister.

Back in my room, I summoned all my courage and knelt to check that he was still there… and I had not completely lost my mind. To my profound relief and equal dismay, I found my visitor exactly where I had left him: slumbering in a frail pile beneath my bed. I stood up to resume chewing on my already bloodied nailbeds.

What was I supposed to do?

How would I keep him hidden?

How would I feed him?

How would I make him *leave*?

I paced for a while, stopped to admonish myself, then paced yet more. In the tales, what I had just done would certainly cost the heroine everything. Wise mortals *never* bargain with The Others. Everyone knew they were a cunning, malicious lot that delighted in human suffering. He could transform into a bear and eat me or curse my entire family to ruin for failing to guess his name. He might snatch me away to his realm where his fellows would make me dance to death for their amusement. Would he drain my life's blood to sustain himself, or ravage me to produce a changeling child who would bring doom to the whole kingdom?

"He might wish to sleep without your noisome thoughts prattling around the room," his tiny voice drifted up from the floor.

I yelped.

"You can hear my thoughts?" I screeched after several gulping breaths.

"Only the incredibly loud ones." He sighed. "Right now, you are an orchestra, entire."

I wasn't sure what an orchestra was, but I knelt to see him better. He had shifted to his other side and was now facing me.

Brida, but he was ugly. The skin around his eyes was pitted and black like a bruised apple. His lips were thin and sunken around his gums. The spiderwebbing of hair at his crown was nearly white and insubstantial as crumbling lace.

"Who are you?" I asked.

"I have many names," he answered.

I fidgeted. "So… then, you are…O- Other?"

He sniffed, wrinkling his liver-spotted nose. "Have you known many men trapped within a scroll?"

"No," I replied without guile.

"Well, you have your answer," he said, his tone patronizing.

Aside from abject terror, a tinge of irritation flared in my gut. Although I was not stupid, I *was* painfully naive. I hadn't known many men at all save my father and a handful of his servants. Girls like me lived in a prison of needlepoint, linens, and housework. We did not get out much. His response, while accurate, was a little unfair.

"Forgive me. That was perhaps in poor taste."

Well, at least he wasn't rude.

I fidgeted more.

"What, erm, what should I call you?"

He seemed to consider that for a while.

"You may call me Briar, for that is what my mother called me, long ago."

I was honestly shocked to hear one such as he should have a mother. I imagined all the fey-folk sprang from the ground fully-grown and predisposed to mischief.

His laugh was dry. "You've heard many tall tales, I see."

I had no retort, for it was true.

Instead, I said, "My name is Deirdre."

"I know."

I squinted at him. "You hear more of my thoughts than you say."

Hc gave a grotesque sort of smirk.

"You are the only one who visits the Roman archive besides your father and the librarian tasked with keeping it clean. I have heard servants speak your name, and know you are the eldest daughter of the adversary."

"Adversary? But my father is King of Ulaid."

He made a rough sound in his tiny throat.

"No mortal man rules Emain Macha, my dear."

I simply stared back at him, having no idea what he was talking about. My father was king, as his father, and his before him had been.

"If my father isn't king, who is?"

Briar said nothing for a while, just stared.

I squirmed a bit. Perhaps he would eat me after all? I had no idea how I would defend myself since I was the fool who set him free. I resumed my furious fidgeting.

"How were you trapped in that scroll?"

"The Romans have strong gods."

"The Romans? But they've all gone," I said, breathily. "And as far as I know, they only have the one God."

The little fellow's face fell. "One god?"

"Aye, the Nailed God. His priests come calling each winter, but Father has forbidden their teachings."

"Has he?"

"Well, yes. He says their kind spread indolence and fear. King Mark of Kernow has them whipped whenever they trespass his realm, or worse. But my father says he and the Pendragon of Wales are the sole holdouts. Most of the Britons have already bent the knee to their leader in Rome."

"The Nailed God," the little man repeated, mystified.

I drew myself up a little. "You've been in that scroll a long time, haven't you?"

"My foe was a man named Agricola."

I'd read of this Agricola and his half-hearted attempts at conquering Ulaid for her timber. Since we Eireans had no written language of our own, everything we knew of the outer world was painted into scrolls in either Latin or Greek. My father had both languages, but I only had a working knowledge of the Roman tongue. Thankfully, most of my father's library was stacked high with the latter. While I never mastered the language, I could read it— which was more than most men and women I knew could boast of.

According to my reading, after many skirmishes and tribal uprisings, Agricola finally gave up the isle as a "tractless waste," returning to the more civilized Britannia to the east. But this was many centuries ago, and now the land of Briton was once more divided into squabbling kingdoms who raided and slaughtered each other in a ceaseless cycle of unending violence and greed.

I did the sums in my head to the best of my knowledge and inhaled sharply.

"But that was six hundred turns ago!"

He appeared to arrive at the same conclusion I did, going nearly translucent as whatever blood he had further leached from his skin. He uttered something harsh in a tongue I did not recognize.

"Leave me." He coughed.

A moment later, I realized he was weeping.

I fumbled under my mantle to produce the linen kerchief Cook had given me earlier and unraveled two beautiful bannock cakes stuffed with currents and honey. I shuffled forward on my knees to place the cakes within his reach.

"I have nowhere to go," I said, softly. "But I will be quiet." Climbing into my bed above, I tucked myself into my furs, my mind keeping pace with the pounding of my heart. Despite my mistrust of him, I was genuinely sorry for him.

How could I evict someone who'd suffered as much as he clearly had? I'd never heard a man weep so, or had it affect me so deeply. Such sadness was a marrow-deep, soul-shredding affair. Before long, wet, salty tears rolled down my own cheeks.

"Cook will come soon to check on me, so you must stay out of sight."

It took him a while to answer, his high, gravelly voice dry. "I understand."

"And," I went on, summoning all my remaining courage, "please don't hurt me."

I fell asleep waiting for his answer.

COOK DID COME LATER, AND AS PROMISED, SHE BROUGHT my mother's things with her. With her finger over her lips, she crammed the items deep into my trunk. I gave her a wordless nod, praying she wouldn't spy the guilt written all over my face. After she'd fussed over me for a good half an hour and stuffed my face full of mutton stew and cranberry jam, she finally took her leave.

Never once had she looked down to discover the cunning creature under my bed, may Brida be praised. She did, however, leave a clean chamber pot and another parcel of tarts. The former made me blush, knowing I now had an audience to hide from. The latter, I was sure, my guest would be grateful for. When she'd gone, I leapt out of bed and slid onto my knees to search for him.

He was gone.

All that remained was the linen napkin I'd left for him, bereft of tarts. And the now-empty scroll.

A nearly overwhelming relief surged through me.

I buried my face in my fur rug, thanking Brida, Macha, and even Mabh for this small mercy. Perhaps setting him free had been the right thing to do? Perhaps he'd find his way home to his people, to his rightful place. I hoped for his sake, and mine, this was the case. I got up, wiping tears from the corner of my eyes.

Now that that was done, I could get back to worrying about the midsummer tourney; planning my escape from my sister's shadow. A task better suited to a girl not plagued by madness.

A girl so lonely, she missed her strange visitor only slightly less than she feared him.

Five

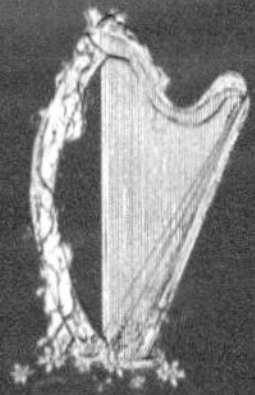

In the weeks after I had avoided becoming a cautionary tale for future generations, my father's guests began to arrive. Most Eirean kingdoms and clanlands celebrated the midsummer, but generally spent the most effort at Beltane or Lughnasa, but in Ulaid, our legends placed particular emphasis on the solstice.

Of course, it was midsummer when Macha, our patron goddess, was forced to run her race. If you don't know the story, it goes something like this…

In the light of the midsummer moon

King Conor of Ulaid had bought several fine horses

Renowned for their speed and beauty

Unmatched, they had no equal

Conor invited his warriors and landsmen to a great feast

A venue to please the gods

A contest to speed tales of his might

But one of his landsmen had better luck than he

Crunden, the landsman was called

Had been most blessed of all

His wife was the goddess Macha in human form

And an oath he did swear, to never speak of her to the king

Nor his men

Nor his druids

At the feast, the men boasted of their wives' loyalty

Crunden held his tongue

The men boasted of their wives' skills

Crunden kept his council

The men boasted of their wives' beauty

Crunden bit his cheek

But then King Conor described his horses

And claimed none could match their speed

Here, Crunden forgot his oath

He boasted that his wife could beat the king's horses

On foot

Offended, King Conor demanded Crunden produce his wife

Or Crunden would forfeit his life

King Conor's men dragged Crunden's wife from their hut

*And lo, she was as beautiful, intelligent, and spry as he had
boasted. But heavily with child*

Conor spake Crunden's shame

He bade Macha race

With disdain, Macha declared that the king had no right

All men born of a woman must respect a woman with child

But Conor would not hear her

She would race his horses on foot

Or Crunden would die

Macha warned the king that he would regret his pride

But raced she did

And won

But the race was too much for Macha's mortal body

She birthed her twins on the plain

Stone dead, in a wash of blood and grief

And just before her human body gave out

She leveled a finger at Conor's heart

'For your pride, the men of Ulaid will ever be the warriors,
strongest warriors of the realm'

She spake, and a storm gathered to mark her words.

A great wind swept king and men together, drawing them
close

'But as you have dishonored this female flesh

So shall your warrior's strength fail them

For nine days every moon

For nine generations hence'

'Here shall the men of Ulaid achieve

The renown you so crave.

A promise of greatness

Never to be realized'

And with her curse

And the lifeblood flowing from her mortal form

The sky raged above her head

The ravens circled the field

Crying 'death to Ulaid'

And the men knew what they had done

Macha, the might of war and womanly virtue

Gathered her dead twins to her bosom

And quit the field

Ulaid's doom trailing in her wake

And thus, Emain Macha, the seat of the Kings of Ulaid, was born. My father's fortress stood proudly on the banks of Lough Neagh. An older fort straddled two hills called 'Macha's Twins' nearby, though none but the druids were allowed to venture there. It is said that this place was once used to honor the dead and send appeasements to our angry patroness, but some said it was older than the tale itself, and therefore could not be the seat of the old King Conor.

Nevertheless, my father was King of Ulaid, and his cousin Áed Findliath ruled at Tara. Technically both are still men of Ulaid, but Áed's mother had been the previous High King's daughter, and the natural choice for overruler. My father, as the Lord Ruler of Emain Macha, was still considered the Uí Néill— or highest Uí Néill chieftain.

Again, this was all probably very confusing to any-one who wasn't born in these lands, like my stepmother and her women. They made no secret of their disdain for our heritage, and often gossiped about the weakness of Áed Findliath's claim to the High Kingship and would even say King Ælla had long since made the unpopular ruler his vassal. I wasn't sure about that, but he and his sons were not well loved in Ulaid, regardless of rumor. Many of my father's warriors spoke openly about their desire to elevate my father to High King.

Of course, this is why my father had married Hester in the first place.

With King Ælla in his back pocket, my father need never fear reprisals from Áed Findliath.

Or so he thought, anyway.

In the meantime, I was lost somewhere in the labyrinth of his schemes. I could not claim my rights as the eldest daughter of the Uí Néill of Ulster, nor could I choose my own path. A wheel stuck to its spoke in mud, I was, and far less precious. As the midsummer guests arrived, each with their own panoply of colors, faces, and names— my pride pricked far worse than it ever had.

I had never been beautiful, nor especially wise, nor very talented at the loom. But I had always believed I was at least intelligent, literate, kind, and compassionate. It seemed, these were not virtues the men of

Eire particularly prized. Their eyes skipped over me at the feast each night. I was ignored at the games. They peered past me in the hall. Not a one asked to speak to me, dance with me, or sit beside me during our nightly feasts. By the end of the month, we had nearly forty warriors and lords sleeping in the great hall or camped outside with their men.

None of them paid the least mind to me at all.

Perhaps, dear reader, you live in a land where a woman's life does not depend on the men who claim her. But the best I could hope for was a good match with a kind lord. And as the daughter of a king, I should have first choice. If not for Calanthe, I would, too. Now, however, my father would choose for me from among her leftovers.

I tried to have faith in my father that his choice would suit me.

But...

There was also the possibility that he could find no match for me at all. If that happened, then I would be sent to the sea, same as the other rejected women. For what good is a woman no man would have? Of course, my father could offer me to a landsman or petty chieftain. I strongly suspected this was to be my fate and did my best to make peace with the notion. Perhaps he'd have a kind manner, know his letters, and have a yearning for the old tales, like me. Perhaps he'd have children already, and a comfortable home with a wide hearth. Perhaps he'd have horses he'd teach me to ride, and a barn full of ewes to nurse each spring. Perhaps he'd smile a lot, and read with me beside the fire each night.

I could make do with such a life.

Could even be happy.

If I survived this unending indignity, that is.

I wouldn't paint myself as especially vain or proud, but every woman has her limit.

That morning, as I dressed, I vowed to try a bit harder to stand out on my own merits. I eschewed my mother's far too eye-catching gowns for my best frock but did take Cook's advice about my hair. I braided it at my temples and tied the two together at my nape while allowing the rest to flow freely down my back. I was far from lovely, with my high cheekbones and too-wide mouth, but my hair was pretty enough. I had my mother's raven-dark waves that glowed nearly violet by candlelight. It swept past my bottom in a lustrous dark mass. I appraised my appearance in my bronze glass, and sighed.

With my mother's pearls at my throat, I wasn't half bad. I wore my green linen belted with my mother's gilt-braided belt. The fabric divided at the shoulders to display tapered white sleeves beneath, and then split beneath my belt showing a triangle of chemise to my slippered toes. Before I left, I spied the bell on its leather cord laying still on my larder. Without a good reason why, I picked it up and tied it around my wrist. Maybe it would grant me courage.

When Cook saw me come downstairs, her eyes lit up bright as a star. "Oh, my girl! Don't you look graceful as a swan?"

I twaddled my thumbs, giving her a nervous smile. "Are you sure this isn't a bit much?"

"Don't be silly! Your father will beam with pride."

But I wasn't worried about my father.

I was worried about Hester.

And for good reason.

I came into the hall unescorted.

With no ladies of my own, I had no one to come in with.

Again, not by choice.

At first, no one seemed to notice me winding my way past the benches and braziers toward the east windows that were open to the warm night air. I wasn't brave enough to stride down the center as my sister or stepmother might, so I carefully picked my way around the guests and their gathered weapons, shields, and other trappings. The men with high enough status would sleep here on these benches or tables on each night of the tourney. While Emain Macha was a mighty fortress, it did not have room for nigh on a hundred guests. Most of the men would sleep in the courtyard outside, or in tents just below the walls.

I kept my eyes downcast, very cautious not to call attention to myself. The men here were high lords or their best warriors... the very pinnacle of Eire's fighting elite. But they were loud, crude, and boisterous as any man, high or low. I was nearly to the dais where my father and stepmother were seated, when a large hand closed over my elbow, jerking me back. Into a burly man's lap I fell, flushing scarlet to the roots of my hair.

The fellow had an unkempt red beard and a mean look in his beady brown eyes. He smelled of cheese, ale, and sweat.

"Unhand me this instant," I demanded, covering my nose.

He belched in my face.

His nearby friends crowed at his wit.

"I said, let me go!" I hissed.

"Why should I? You look well enough on my knee."

I struggled free, but his meaty fist closed over my forearm.

"Now, I do like a lass with mettle."

Again, his companions laughed with him.

Another man came up behind me, obscuring me from the dais altogether. If anyone were to glance over, they wouldn't see me at all.

"I am not a serving woman," I protested.

He guffawed, dragging me to the bench again. "Who cares? I like 'em skinny and elf-eyed."

Looking around, none of his companions seemed the least interested in hearing me. He pulled me closer by my waist. I slapped him as hard as I could. First, he blinked at me while the men laughed, but I watched as a dark thing slid behind his smile.

He jerked me forward, snarling, "What's this? You would raise your hand to a king's man?"

"I'd raise a hand to any cur who dared lay hands on a defenseless woman, sir."

He raised his hand again. Once I was sure he meant to strike me, a voice cut through the din.

"Cormac! If you mean to insult the Uí Néill, you couldn't do much better than by pawing at his eldest daughter."

The ogre blanched and let go of me so quickly, I might have burned him.

He shot to his feet and bowed, red cheeks blazing purple. "Please forgive me, my lady! I didn't recognize you."

I backed away, rubbing my sore arm, more cross than I'd been in years. Several ugly bruises were bound to bloom there later.

"I hope you lose every bout, you ugly bear."

His companions laughed while I turned away.

This was how I met *him*.

A man more beautiful than any I'd ever spied smiled sheepishly at me and bent his knee.

"Máel Sechnaill, at your service, my lady."

I blinked at him for quite some time, uncertain where my tongue had gone.

This was the erstwhile High King's younger brother? Everyone in my father's household called *this* man a stuttering dolt? He had lustrous golden-brown locks that framed his jaw when he smiled. His eyes were the undaunted blue of a cloudless sky.

He held out a hand.

"May I escort you to the dais?"

I stared at his open palm like it might be filled with leeches.

No one had ever asked for my hand before.

After an uncomfortably long while, I stretched my fingers out, inch by inch, until he gently tucked my arm into his. He wasn't much taller than me, as I was fairly tall for a woman. His warmth was unsettling. Did all men exist at such temperatures? I had no idea. I knew I was flushing, and flushed the more. I stole a glance at him from the corner of my eye and my ears burned. His jaw held light stubble four shades darker than his hair, the tattoos over his brow marking his highborn status. Only lords, princes, and kings bore these precious ogham sigils. I repressed a shiver.

He led me to the dais steps where Calanthe and her mother waited, both staring.

Máel bent me a curt bow with another blinding smile. My heart sailed directly into my throat.

"Till next time then, Lady Deirdre."

I was halfway to my seat at the far end of the dais, before I realized I'd never told him my name.

Six

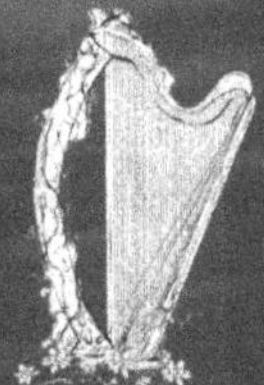

The evening sped past my eyes swift as an arrow. My sister was introduced to the waiting guests as expected, looking radiant and golden in her finely-woven, berry-dyed linen gown. Hester was equally resplendent in gold and cream, her fillet and torc gleaming brilliantly in the torchlight. Every now and then her scowl would pin me to the edge of the dais, doing its level best to shrink me to scale. My father's dark head towered over everyone else at the center of the dais in the highest chair, his booming voice and raucous good cheer traveling the length and breadth of the hall for well over two hours. His grizzled cheeks were wine-bright, dark eyes glowing with merriment. There were few things my father loved more than a feast, save maybe a feast during a tourney in his honor. As for Calanthe, she sat primly at the center of the dais at her mother's right hand, behaving beautifully and drawing every male eye in attendance, save one.

Máel stood well within my range of vision. I wouldn't dare to look his way, but I felt his eyes on me, move with me. I had never been stared at so blatantly before and had no idea where to shift my attention. Feeling my plate might be the safest place to point my burning cheeks, I kept my head down.

When the feasting was over, the women were generally excused before the men drank themselves blind. My father was already shoulder-deep in his cups when Hester finally stood, tugging my sister up beside her. The men collectively groaned watching their quarry take her leave. Calanthe giggled with her maids as Hester prodded her toward the rear stairs. Hester paused at the door only long enough to mark me on the far side of the dais.

Soon, her gaze promised.

I swallowed.

I knew her well enough to know she would make me pay for my boldness, by one means or another. Taking her leaving as my own cue to depart, I followed at a sedate pace past my father's chair. I made it only part way when that chair dragged sideways to find my father's grinning face staring down at me. I froze, unsure what was happening.

"Deirdre!" he boomed, red-faced and reeking of ale. "There's someone you should meet."

I had time to squawk a "Who—" when I was spun about to face the High King's brother once more.

Máel's disarming smile captured me mid-spin. I caught the arm of my father's chair, rather than spill into the rushes, my skin burning brighter than the nearest brazier.

"Hello, my lady."

"Hello." I curtsied back.

Glancing behind him, his friend Cormac was conspicuously absent.

"Máel here is my cousin Áed's half-brother, Daughter," my father said. "He asked to meet you, 'specially."

He said the last jovially, but I detected a note of warning.

My father was never as drunk as he seemed.

He told me once that a king could not rule from the bottom of a tankard, and that any king who did, would never rule long. Since he'd been the Uí Néill for nearly two decades, I'd say he was rather wise.

I had no idea what to say.

"It is a pleasure to meet you, my lord."

Máel's blue, blue eyes met and held mine.

"I assure you, the pleasure is mine."

My father turned to me.

"My daughter is quite well read, Lord Sechnaill. She has had the benefit of Suetonius, Marcus Aeurelius, and even Ovid, if I remember correctly."

"Is that so, my lady?"

I fought hard to keep the blush from my cheeks, but it was a losing battle. Ovid had penned a great many love poems, many of them quite scandalous, indeed. I had read a few, which made me blush, but also boasted that I was better read than most of the men in Eire.

"Yes," I answered. Waiting for the inevitable 'that's very odd' commentary. This was not strictly ladylike behavior. The reading that is, not the love poems.

"I have never read Ovid, nor Aurelius. I fear my Latin leaves much to be desired." Máel grinned. "Perhaps my lady would be so kind as to grant me a tour of your father's collection while we are here? With a chaperone, of course," he added, for my father's benefit. "Your Majesty's library is well lauded at Tara."

My father chuckled good-naturedly but I could see the cogs turning in his dark head.

"I am pleased to hear it, cousin. Deirdre and I would be delighted to grant this request."

My head snapped around.

We would be?

What was happening?

My father's expression spared no hint of his intentions.

Máel beamed, bowed, and placed a hand over his heart. His chestnut curls gleamed slightly copper in the light of a nearby brazier. "Til then, my lady."

He and his party retreated back to the far wall, the site of my recent mortification.

I noticed his friend Cormac, twisting his ugly red head around to leer at me on their way.

But I didn't have time to reiterate my fervent wish that he lose every bout. My father steered me toward the door, gripping my elbow hard lest I turn around once more. It wasn't until we were through to the other side that he let his mask slip.

"That arrogant fop! How *dare* he present himself in my house."

My stomach sank.

"What do you mean, Father?"

A hideously deep scowl carved itself into his already sharp jaw. "That bastard Áed sent him to spy, of course."

It took a moment, but this cold logic managed to worm its way through my overheated ears.

Ah. That explains things.

Máel's smile was not for me, after all.

Of course not. I deflated a bit as my father pulled me upward toward the royal apartments. I allowed myself to be led, my hair forming a curtain to hide my disappointment.

"Whatever happens, Deirdre, you must not let that man near your sister. Do you hear me?"

He paused to give me a very hard stare.

"King Ælla is at odds with Áed, as the latter means to purge the Nords from these shores once and for all."

I remembered myself, clearing my throat. My father did not suffer moon-faced nonsense from anyone but my sister.

Least of all me.

He expected me to answer when spoken to, and I, as ever, was a dutiful daughter.

"But Calanthe is Ælla's grand-niece. He wouldn't dare harm her."

I could have applauded myself for my even, unbothered tone.

"No, he wouldn't, but he might wish to steal her for his brother."

My brows drew inward. "Father, he couldn't even if he wished to. There are a hundred warriors in the hall tonight."

All we ever talked about was Calanthe.

All anyone ever thought about was Calanthe.

And now it seemed, even the very first man who'd ever smiled at me, was there for Calanthe, too.

I very much wished to be elsewhere.

"Mind what I told you, Daughter." He turned away toward his own chamber down the hall and up the stairs.

"What if he decides it's me he wants, Father?" I asked before he got too far away.

"Well, he'd be a fool to choose so unwisely, wouldn't he? Áed would never resist the opportunity to thumb his nose at Ælla for such sport. Mark me, he's come to take her back with him, by whatever means."

"He would make an enemy of our house so easily?"

He winked, turning away. "A woman worth having, is one worth stealing."

His laughter rang through the halls.

I WAS FULLY IN TEARS BY THE TIME I MADE IT BACK TO MY room. I threw myself onto the bed and sobbed. No matter what I did, Calanthe won. I could have nothing for myself.

Nothing.

No one.

The only man who'd ever seemed to see me, my father was convinced would kidnap my sister at the first opportunity. Of course he would try. He was the High King's brother. If he couldn't win her hand, he'd take her. She *was* the niece of the most powerful ruler in Eire, and the daughter of his chief rival. Máel was only there to broker an exchange, not to make eyes at me. Even if he did favor me, his brother would choose his wife for him, same as my father would eventually choose mine. On such a list, I would never rank.

I had to have the worst luck in the Ulaid.

I should have pleaded ill or fallen down the stairs. Maybe I could avoid the next week of feasts and contests if I sucked down a sleeping potion or drowned myself in the bath. But Calanthe would find a way to drag me out for her benefit. Or my father would send me to the sea for refusing to be dutiful.

I wanted the earth to swallow me.

I wanted to walk into the lough and never come up.

I wanted to be free of this place.

"Well," said a slightly tinny voice from somewhere nearby. "Those are many feelings to process all at once."

I scrambled upright with a scream.

At least I'd meant to scream, but the sound simply wouldn't push past my lips. A raspy whisper rattled through my teeth instead. Bemused, I clutched at my throat while my cunning fellow emerged from a shadowy corner in my room.

He was just as ugly as before, but cleaner, and more… *something*, somehow.

I had a moment of panic.

I *knew* he hadn't gone!

I recoiled in fear, but he raised a hand.

"That's enough theatrics for now, my dear. Will you promise to behave?"

I gulped air like a flopping fish for several moments until I felt ridiculous. Eventually, I nodded in defeat. My voice returned with a hard groan.

I covered my throat and glared. "Why did you do that?"

"With a hundred warriors in the hall, I'd rather avoid the resulting clamor."

My eyes narrowed. "Why have you come back?"

He crossed his arms and paced the room. His skin looked as pale and fragile as ever, though his liver spots had faded.

He looked like a cross old beggar, if I were being honest.

He glared.

I bit my lip, remembering I needed to keep my thoughts to myself.

"I owe you," he grumbled unhappily. "And I never shirk a debt."

I was sure I hadn't heard him correctly.

"You owe *me*?"

"Yes. You have no idea the fate you spared me, the torture you wrenched me from. This is a debt I cannot carry to Tír na nÓg."

He stared at me for a while as if waiting for me to say something.

For the dozenth time that evening, I was at a loss for words.

"I'm sure you owe me nothing," I said, finally.

He threw up his hands.

"See! That's why I can't let it rest. No other mortal would pass on a chance to indebt one such as me."

I shivered at the thought.

"I don't want you to owe me anything, nor do I need anything."

He stroked his chin while he observed me. "Nothing, you say?"

I watched his too green eyes track over my loose black hair and the pearls at my throat.

I looked down. "My father hopes to catch a large dowry for my sister. We must all play our part."

"Yet," he said slowly. "She has usurped your place."

"Yes, but it's not her fault. Her mother is Norse."

"I am learning of these Northmen. Fearsome fighters, if uncultured."

"Calanthe's great uncle is their king of kings, Ælla."

"Ælla," he rolled the name around on his tongue. "He is rich, famous?"

"Oh, aye. He owns half of Eire and all of Northumbria. He's a fearsome man, to be sure."

"So, your fair sister is first because her great-uncle is this fancy man?"

I shrugged. "I haven't heard it put quite that way, but yes."

His eyes were brighter tonight than they were when we first met.

Perhaps he was shaking off the pall of death.

"How did Agricola trap you in the scroll," I asked.

"As if I'd tell another human soul."

I laughed and he watched me, seemingly fascinated.

I cleared my throat and took a seat in my window box.

"What would you have of me, sir?"

"First, I would have you call me Briar, as I told you before."

I smiled. "Fine. What would you have of me, Briar?"

"It is not what I would have of you, but what you should accept from me."

"What's it to be then, a comb that sings me to sleep? A perfume that makes all men love me at first sight?"

He smirked. "What if I told you that anything your heart desires could be yours?"

"I would ask you what it would cost me."

"You are not the trusting sort."

"No."

"I could make you Queen of Eire."

I flinched. "Gods, no. You've never met the High King, Áed."

He cursed in the same language I'd heard him speak before.

The vowels sounded very familiar, as if hearing someone speak in passing, without catching the gist of their conversation.

"Fate's teeth, woman. What *will* you take?"

I laughed, dryly. "Will you grant me three wishes, then?"

He didn't hesitate. "Done."

I gasped. "I didn't mean it!"

"Too late."

"No," I said, standing up. "Please take it back, I don't want—"

"But be careful what you wish for, this magic is older than anything you can possibly dream... even I have no control over the path it takes."

"I don't *want* it!" I cried. "Take it back."

Quick as a serpent's strike, the leather cord with the bell tightened around my wrist. Before my eyes, the cord melted and reformed, gold and silver tendrils creeping across my wrist to form an elegant chain. The bell, once a dull flat bronze, took on a glowing yellow sheen.

Such a beautiful gift.

I was horrified.

He rubbed his hands together and splayed them wide.

"I can't. The deal is struck. No harm if you use them wisely."

He walked back toward the darkest corner of my room.

"Wait!" I flung a hand out, as if they would stop him. "Please don't—"

He turned back just as he melted into the shadows, his smirk illuminated by the fire in my hearth.

"I will come if you call my name."

Then he was gone.

Seven

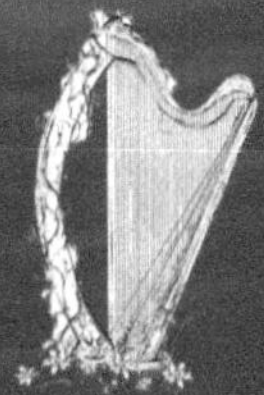

I fretted through the next day, and the one after. I'd taken to wearing long sleeves so no one would spot the golden charm on my wrist, although it was balmy as midsummer in the hall. How would I explain where such a fine thing had come from? I had never owned any jewels or baubles like this. My stepmother or her women would surely accuse me of theft. But, the chain wouldn't come off. I couldn't roll it down my wrist and there was no clasp to speak of. Worse, it would neither bend nor break and was far too tight to slip off. In a panic, I snuck downstairs at dawn to nick some lard from the kitchens. No one was usually about at that hour or would hardly notice me digging around in the pantry.

Or so I thought.

In my state, I'd completely forgotten about the guests in the hall. Of course Cook and her minions would be up before dawn, preparing the day's feasts. I cursed myself under my breath, a habit it seems I'd inherited from Briar.

Wiping her hands on her apron, Cook gave a start when she saw me. I attempted to back out of the room and run upstairs, but she caught my sleeve. "Why are you about so early, my lady?"

Like a starved fox, I leapt at the first thought that crossed my mind.

"I was hoping there were parsnip tarts leftover from last night."

She pursed her lips. "Couldn't sleep?"

I shook my head, eyes downcast.

I hated to lie to her as she was the only kind person in my life, but I knew better than to share my misfortune. Folk were deathly afraid of The Others in Ulaid. Remember, our city was founded by a curse. She would most definitely revile me, did she learn of my misdeed. They all would.

In Eire, bad luck was a plague worse than pox.

Cook filled a kerchief with the tarts I'd requested along with a hardboiled egg. "I'll have Taryn bring you some porridge after the men are fed in the hall." She sniffed. Cook was no lover of men, especially boastful warriors who manhandled her staff. "Best you steer well clear of them, lass," she warned. I agreed with her wholeheartedly. Hadn't I learned as much yesterday? The men scattered throughout my father's hall in various stages of drunken collapse, would paw at any woman who ventured too close. I felt for Cook's staff. They were in for a very long week, indeed.

While I would be expected to attend feasts and to chaperone my sister if any serious suitors presented themselves, I meant to keep to my room night and day. Munching on one of the tarts she'd given me, I folded the remainder in my mantle and headed for the stairs. My foot had scarcely scraped the first step before four grooms came barreling past me, hauling buckets bound for my stepmother's rooms.

Rather than be flattened or elbowed down the stairs, I elected to take the main stairs across from the great hall. I couldn't believe so many people sleeping, dallying, or working under our roof had slipped my mind. The sun had barely touched the sky, and already grooms and maids buzzed around me like drones in a hive.

Gnawing on my tart, I gingerly stepped around one fellow who carried a bundle of arrows bound for the tiltyard. Another came rushing past half-dragging a clanking sack filled with yew and ash bows. I dodged them both, but watched after them for a moment. Today's contest was to be archery, then? I had always enjoyed watching my father's men at target practice. Archery was one of the few sports women were allowed to engage in. I certainly had no gift for it, but enjoyed it, nonetheless. Calanthe hadn't taken to it, either, and Hester reviled arms altogether. I did gain some satisfaction knowing that if I decided to watch the day's sport, I needn't worry about them for a few hours. I spun back around toward the stairs, chewing my tart and smiling to myself.

And there he was again, grinning.

I stopped, nearly choking on my tart.

Máel bowed at the waist, ever the courtier.

"My lady, you look radiant this morn."

Now I knew he was a liar. There were crumbs on my face, deep circles I could feel (you know the sort) under my eyes, and wild hair that refused to be tamed by a meager braid. I was wearing the same dress I'd worn the night before to boot.

I told myself I liked him less for his obvious flattery.

Rolling my eyes, I nodded politely and stepped around him. "My lord." I sighed, choosing to avoid him.

He dashed up the stairs ahead of me in order to lean against the oak balustrade and smile down at me.

"You are very quick, you know."

I heard my father's voice in my head and paused long enough to cast him a deep frown.

"Do you always haunt the halls at daybreak, my lord?"

He laughed.

It warmed my toes, despite my best efforts to remain unmoved. Áed was wise to send him here. He fairly oozed charm.

"I might ask you the same."

"Hm," I muttered noncommittally, resuming my progress upward. Again, he darted past me, intent to block my exit. I huffed, swallowing the remainder of my tart, forcing a deep blush back whence it came through sheer will alone.

This man wasn't here for me, I reminded myself. He would use me to get to my sister, and through her, my father. He was not someone I should be talking to.

"Have I offended you in some way, lady?" He cocked his head, his deep blue eyes filled with concern.

"Not at all," I lied. "I have much to do today, if you'll pardon me." I shifted to his right and squeezed past. Once more, he sprang ahead, spreading his arms wide to block my path.

I exhaled hard through my nose.

"Whoa, whoa! I *have* offended you somehow. How can I make amends?"

I crossed my arms.

"Calanthe will be down for breakfast in the hall. You needn't chase her through me."

He blinked back at me, apparently stunned.

Exasperated, I refused to be swayed further.

I shoved past him and had made it around the corner when he skidded to a stop ahead of me again. This time, I growled, "What now? I have things to do that—"

"May we start over, Lady Deirdre?" He extended his hand as if to an equal. "My name is Máel, not Áed."

That gave me pause.

"But you are here on his behalf."

He inhaled and leaned against the wall. "Yes, as are many others here for their chieftains. Will you hold that against me? The blood of the great boogeyman Ælla is a strong lure for powerful men."

My molars ground together. "Then, you are wasting time on the wrong sister. Please excuse me."

But he wouldn't let me pass.

His cerulean gazes filled my vision.

> "'*The sharp thorn*
>
> *Often produces*
>
> *Delicate roses…*'"

I couldn't help but look up then. I quoted back,

> "'*You can learn from anyone*
>
> *Even your enemy.*'"

A slow, delighted smile spread over his face.

"Not all men are blind, passionless fools, lady."

I backed up, feeling slightly dizzy.

"Clearly, you lied about Ovid."

"Clearly, you lied about your Latin."

We stared each other down for several heartbeats, frozen in time. Another groom rushed past us, dragging trunks down the hall to my stepmother's chamber. If I weren't so distracted, I'd wonder what in the world the women were doing that needed so many trunks and buckets? Máel backed off slightly but remained a hand's breadth away.

I cleared my throat. "My sister—"

"Is a child. A pretty child, I'll warrant, but a child, just the same."

"But you, like all The Others, aren't here for the daughter of a clanswoman."

He blew air over his lip. "My brother wants her for the thorn she'd thrust into Ælla's side, true. I will pay your father handsomely for her hand, true. She will be Queen of Eire, unless your father is a fool."

I held a breath, keeping my eyes downcast. "And you?"

He leaned down so I couldn't miss his expression.

"I am free to make my own choice."

"That's precisely what every man anywhere says when he means to ruin a naive young girl," Hester's voice carried down the hall.

Máel's head snapped up.

I lurched back as if I'd been struck and rushed around him, face burning.

Hester's icy gaze speared me to the spot.

"Inside. Now," she hissed through her teeth.

For once, I was grateful she had been watching. Máel was a dangerous man, just as my father had warned. I ducked beneath her arm and stood behind her in her open door. Máel tried his smile on her, but it withered when he realized she was not to be trifled with.

He smoothed the front of his tunic. "My apologies, Highness. I meant no disrespect."

Hester scoffed. "That's precisely what you said to me yesterday when my daughter dangled at the end of your hook."

I winced so hard I thought I might bruise something.

Hester looked back at me with a pointed sort of sympathy. "And she has also been advised that you are not to be taken seriously. I hope, for your sake, my lord, you mean to quit this place before the sport turns ugly."

Her message couldn't have been more plain.

I watched him nod, smile that winsome smile, albeit deflated. He left without a backward glance.

I felt... stupid.

Obviously, Hester thought so too. She grabbed my arm and pushed me into her rooms where a bath and breakfast had been laid out for her and Calanthe, although I didn't see my younger sister. She must yet have been abed. Hester dropped me, unceremoniously, into a chair by the fire and shoved a copper tankard in my hand.

"Drink that."

Heedlessly, I obeyed.

And made an immediate face.

Whatever was in there tasted like sweetened charcoal.

My fingers warmed considerably though, which was nice enough.

"Before my daughter rises for the day's nonsense, I think it's time you and I understood each other."

She stared down at me, her dressing robes drawn tight against her fragile frame, wheat-blonde hair spilling over her shoulders. She had been as beautiful as

Calanthe once, I was sure. Perhaps more so. "None of these men are here for you."

"I know that."

"Do you? I saw you wearing your mother's pearls last night, and now someone has been in here pilfering from her things."

"They're mine by right."

She shrugged. "Perhaps soon, but not yet. You are unmarried and have no prospects. Until then, these things belong here. Am I understood?"

I didn't answer. She had no right to keep my mother's things from me.

"You will do as you please, perhaps, but this won't stop my daughter from receiving her due."

I was tired of hearing this.

I looked up.

Whatever she saw in my eyes snapped her mouth shut over her next commandment.

"She has taken *my* place as the eldest daughter of the Uí Néill. All the honors you spend on her were stolen from me."

"It's true, I won't deny it. I know your customs, and I know it is unfair to you."

That was the closest I would ever get to an apology from Hester, I was sure. I willed myself not to cry.

"But it changes nothing. My daughter will be a queen, and you will wed whichever minor lord your father can squeeze the most coin from. This is hardly ideal for you, I realize. So, I vow to do my best for you… after Calanthe is Queen of Eire."

I mulled that over for a while, forcing down angry tears.

"You mean for her to marry Áed?"

She gave me a long hard look that hinted I should guess again.

"No." I sucked in a breath. "You mean for her to marry Máel. But why?"

She shrugged and sat down. "The High King is a fierce soldier but a terrible statesman. His people loathe him, and the clans barely support him. My uncle has sought many treaties with him, all of which he has broken. Máel is loved by all, for obvious reasons."

He *was* inordinately charming.

"If your uncle wants the crown, why doesn't he just take it?"

Ælla could.

He was probably the only one with the men and arms.

"Because until our people are one with yours they will never accept a foreign ruler. Rebellion runs deep in Eire," she remarked dryly. "My mother used to tell me Eireans are weaned on malcontent and indignation. If my uncle takes this isle by force, he would need to stay, and he cannot, for our people must come first."

She meant that Ælla was spread too thin between Northumberland and Daneland. He may have a strong foothold in Dubh-Lin and Corcaigh, but his commanders had failed every attempt to take Tara or make inroads here in Ulaid or the West. Our fighters were stronger than the High King's, and better organized. Apparently, Ælla now had a better plan. Why take by force what you can subvert from the inside? Ælla wanted Áed out of the way. Supporting his more popular brother by giving him his niece would do that rather neatly.

"Father will never let it happen. He is furious that the king's brother should have dared come here."

"Your father may say what he likes, but he won't go to war for Áed. Áed has asked many times."

I set my cup down on the mantle and let out a long breath.

"Fine. I don't care about Áed, Ælla, or Máel," I prevaricated. "Who Calanthe weds is not my concern."

Hester didn't look away. "The prince is a man, Deirdre. He may pour honeyed words into more than one eager ear and mean none of what is said. Calanthe believes he is in love with her already."

My stomach soured.

Of course she did.

"That is her misfortune."

Her eyes were steady.

"He will not take you over Calanthe, Deirdre. Don't believe yourself of more import than you are. It amuses him to play with each of you. A jest among men. But don't doubt for a moment, he is here for the grandniece of his enemy. Not an insignificant princess of no great worth or beauty."

I nodded, not trusting myself to speak.

This wasn't the first time she'd spoken like this to me, but it had never stung so much.

"Perhaps you think I am cruel," she said, folding her hands. "I won't profess to love you any more than you love me, but I will never lie to you. I would be your ally if you'd let me be." She stood, arching her shoulders. "I would have you know, I never wanted to come here. I never chose your father. He was chosen for me. If it were my choice, Calanthe would take her vows across the sea where my people are strong. But the choice is not mine, nor yours, nor even your father's, in the end."

Eight

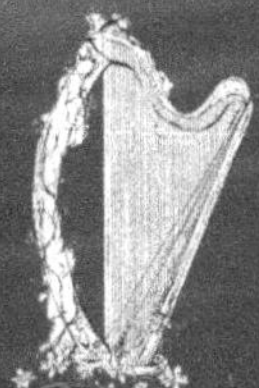

The next day, I skipped the archery contest altogether, pleading illness rather than be forced to endure the feast that night. Instead, I spent the evening alternating between sullen tears and pointed rage. I stalked one end of my chamber to the other, imagining throttling Hester, tearing my sister's golden hair out, and tossing the High King's brother from the nearest window. I imagined poisons, knives, and abrupt tumbles down long flights of stairs.

In some of my waking dreams I held the knife to my sister's throat, and in others, Máel did.

In some, I reversed that order.

In yet more, I summoned a great serpent from the lough outside and laughed as it crushed all of Emain Macha beneath its scaly hide. As the anger left me, I lay upon my bed staring up at my bed curtains and imagining Máel's blue gaze was mine alone. His hand would take mine, his lips would graze my knuckles, and he would smile at me… only me.

Then, he would pull me into his arms, his lips upon my brow.

I turned over, burying my face in my pillow.

As Hester had said, I was neither beautiful nor important. What would a man with such an easy smile want with a wife who would never properly know how? I wept for the hundredth time that day and hated myself for it.

"What silly standards your people have nowadays," said a familiar voice to my right.

I scrambled upward, wiping water and snot from my face.

There, in my window-box, sat my cunning man, his legs outstretched, his arms crossed. His liver spots were gone and his skin looked a deal less puckered than before. He wore a white tunic trimmed in fine silver thread that was far too loose around his skeletally thin frame. But his cobweb-colored hair did appear to be coming in at his scalp again, and his eyes no longer seemed two blackened pits.

"Where did you come from?" I asked, getting rather tired of him popping up whenever he felt like it.

He rolled a shoulder. "Seemed like you were about to make a wish, and I figured you might need council."

"You're wrong," I grumbled, hugging my knees.

"No?" he asked, tilting his head. "Summoning a dragon to drown a city for your hurt pride seems completely reasonable."

I sucked in a breath. "Could I do that?"

"No."

I exhaled through my nose. "What's the point of having three wishes if you won't give me what I want anyway?"

"Were such wishes granted, would that truly make you happy?"

Oh, yes, I thought with a wry smile.

For a time.

I shot him an unkind look. "Would you go away? I want to be alone."

"So you can brood?"

"So I can think!" I snapped.

"Hm," he said, his eyes far too knowing for my tastes. "I think you might waste my gift on a worthless man."

"I would not."

"Hm," he repeated. "They are your wishes to waste. But if I were you, I would make them count."

"You told me you could make me Queen of Eire!"

"And that's what you want? To wed Áed Findliath?"

I chewed my lower lip.

"His brother, Máel, then?"

I looked away, cheeks burning.

He chuckled. "All it took was a few sweet words, eh?"

"What would you know about anything?"

He leaned forward, his smirk infuriating. "I know that Áed will not lose his title, and your charming fellow will never sit his brother's throne."

"How do you know that?"

He sucked his teeth at me. "I know much that you don't, child."

"I am not a child."

"No? You have saved a great king from eternal torment and thereby earned his loyalty— but you haven't the first clue what to do with that gift. You'd spend your grace on meaningless whims rather than use it to improve your lot… nor anyone else's."

"What would you prefer I spend my wishes on, then? Since you are so all-knowing."

He tapped a finger to his nose. "A good girl would wish for her sister's happiness. A smart girl would wish for the happiness of all she holds dear, including herself. And a brave girl would wish for the power to see her own faults and improve upon them."

My ears sprouted flames.

"Then I am selfish, undutiful, and vain."

"I did not say that."

"I would like you to leave now."

We glared at each other through my bed curtains for a while in irritable silence.

"Before I do as you bid, hear me, Deirdre Uí Néill… no good comes from a self-serving act of defiance."

I covered my ears and turned away, lest he impart any more 'wisdom' upon his leaving.

When I finally looked up, he was gone.

But his words lingered long after.

I was angry.

I was tired.

I was indignant.

I was saddened.

I was unseen.

I wanted to be more than that.

I wanted to be important, desired, special.

Why should my sister write my history?

Was it only her birth and pretty face that was to seal my fate, or could I be more? I got up and moved to my larder where my bronze mirror perched on its pestle. A thin face with high cheekbones stared back at me. My eyes were a dark evergreen at twilight. My hair, same as my mother's, was a rich, deep black, kissed here and there by fire.

These were at least arresting features, if not fashionable.

The men of Eire prized fair maidens with flaxen locks and brilliant eyes of blue or warm hazel. I was thin and angular, where Calanthe was soft and pliant. She had a round face with rosy cheeks and dark brows. Hair the color of summer wheat. A full figure with wide hips and round bosoms. She dimpled when she smiled, which was often. She was a small girl, too, with the crown of her head barely scraping my father's collarbone.

On the other hand, my father and I stood nearly eye-to-eye. I was lithe and pale where my sister was fair and bright. My features too sharp to be truly beautiful. Too cool to invite much warmth. I wanted to change that. I wanted to be more.

I wanted to be alluring.

I wanted to be enchanting.

I wanted to be beautiful.

I made my first wish.

THE NEXT MORNING, I CAME DOWNSTAIRS WEAR ING MY mother's silver gown. The dress was quilted linen that I pulled over one of her finer, gossamer-thin chemises that peeked through the corded sleeves and at the divided 'V' beneath my gilded belt. I wore her pearls again, but this time hung a small emerald my father had given her for my first name day from its string, tucking this fincry into the hollow of my throat. I left my hair down again, save for two braids at my temple, to accentuate the height of my cheekbones. I gaped at my reflection in my bronze mirror for some time. The girl I saw there had full red lips that bowed a bit at the center. She had winged black brows that arched over vibrant green eyes fringed by long, thick, black lashes.

Her skin was fair as milk dusted by roses.

Her throat was long and fair and smooth as pearl.

Her hair was a river of ink pouring over her shoulders

The girl I beheld in that polished surface was more than beautiful. She was everything I longed to be.

I smiled at her and she smiled back.

Today, I would be seen.

Today, I would be heard.

Today, I would take what I wanted.

I entered the great hall for breakfast.

Although I feared my heart would burst from my chest, I forced my head up high. A very abrupt hush settled over the gathering as I passed. Conversations dwindled away mid-sentence, eyes went round, tankards spilled. Men elbowed each other, and the maidservants covered their mouths with their hands. Whispers filled the space behind me as I ascended the dais steps, my jaw set.

Hester saw me first, and I was glad to watch her pale.

My father raised a dark brow, confused but not ruffled.

As for Calanthe, she was busy giggling with Máel, who sat on the table facing her, mead in hand. She turned and I watched the color leech from her face when she saw me. I could not describe to you how exquisite a pleasure her expression was for me. I held her eyes for a long while, not hateful, not aggressive… just confident and sure.

Today, I thought, *you will not usurp me.*

Beside her, Máel got to his feet, blinking like he meant to wake from a dream. I ignored him, though I had no doubt I would feel his eyes upon me from then on.

Calanthe frowned.

I smiled and looked away.

"Father," I said, curtsying. It was an action I'd performed a thousand times, but today it was as if we were meeting for the first time.

"Daughter," he said, rubbing his chin. "You're looking hale today, my dear."

I saw him mark my mother's emerald with interest.

"Thank you," I answered. "I'm feeling much better."

"Good, good," he said, motioning me to my place on his left. I lifted my skirts and walked around the table to take my seat, gingerly folding my napkin and retrieving my belt knife to cut a hunk of cheese from the larder.

My father's critical eye never left me.

Nor had anyone else's in the hall, for that matter.

So, this was the power Calanthe had enjoyed all this while. I would be lying if I said I didn't enjoy every moment.

"Hester said you'd taken your mother's things from her room," he said for my benefit alone.

I helped myself to some stewed apples without looking at him.

"She was wrong to keep them from me."

"Hmph," my father muttered, taking a sip of his mead. "I suppose this means war then, no?"

"Yes," I said, chewing. I finally looked at him, noting Hester still as a rod on his other side. "It does."

He chuckled. "Be mindful that you do not disgrace me."

"No, Father."

"And choose your battles wisely."

"Yes, Father."

He snickered to himself, eying the gathering with renewed interest. "If only you'd shown such backbone when you were small, no?"

I chewed my cheek at him, and he chuckled harder.

"Snatch this prize from Ælla and I will reward your intended, handsomely," he whispered behind his hand.

Hester hadn't heard him, but I knew she wasn't stupid.

Only one person in Eire hated the Danes more than High King Áed; my father.

Hester's expression dared me to try.

I could feel Máel's eyes boring into the top of my head.

I smiled into my cup.

"Yes, Father."

Nine

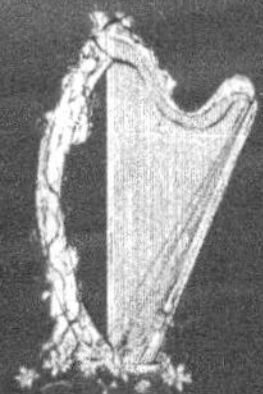

This day was the most delightful I'd spent in my father's keeping. Being that I'd lived in Emain Macha all of my life, you might have some idea of what that meant to me. People had never been more courteous to me, never as kind, concerned, or interested in what I had to say. Men danced attendance on my every whim, be it mead, sweets, or an explanation of the day's contests.

We sat outside under my father's observation tent while the warriors of Ulaid competed at spears in the field below. Those who did not fight sat on benches nearby, swirling tankards and shouting encouragement while they waited their turn. These men spent a good amount of time engaging me in conversation, asking which fighter I thought had the best shield, or what I thought of the weather for our day's sport. Some brought me wildflowers or polished stones taken from the lakebed and tied with ribbon. More simply said 'hello' and stared from some distance, no doubt comparing me to my sister and scratching their chins appraisingly.

Calanthe did not lack for visitors and well-wishers, of course, but I could see a muscle ticking in her soft jaw that told me she didn't appreciate the competition. I was delighted to disappoint her that the world did not, in fact, revolve around her after all.

Although I was having a very good time, Máel had yet to speak to me. I saw him here and there, once at Calanthe's elbow for a time, and again further afield, watching me from afar. Every bit of my strength went into resisting the urge to meet his eyes. Instead, I laughed when prompted, smiled when expected, and otherwise carried myself like the daughter of a king.

I could hear my stepmother grinding her molars to powder nearby, but couldn't care less.

Today, I was my mother's daughter, too.

When the men began to throw, I found myself absorbed.

A dozen targets were constructed in a line at the edge of the hill at varying lengths from the long rope the warriors had gathered behind some paces away. Each blind was constructed with hay covered by black cloth with red lines painted at its centera bullseye. The nearest stood perhaps no more than eight feet from the line, while the furthest was easily two yards away. The warriors gathered, bare-chested, slapping and shoving each other with wide grins. I had never seen so many unclothed men before. Neither had Calanthe. I snuck a glance at her and was relieved to see I wasn't the only one blushing.

Máel emerged from that crowd, and my breath caught.

His corded arms and back gleamed golden in the sunlight, dappled by blue whorls and lines, the marks of his clan. He'd tied his long brown hair back with a leather cord, displaying the fine cut of his jaw, and the dark stubble that made his eyes glow. His teeth flashed white and straight at something one of his fellows had said, and suddenly, his eyes found mine.

His smile faded.

I didn't look away this time.

He nodded at me, then turned to the lists.

The combatants collectively cheered their prince, spears flashing. He stepped up to the line, flexed his back, and raised his spear. He pulled his arm back in a perfect arc, sighting down the balanced point of his left hand. And let fly. And missed. The spear sank harmlessly between the two most distant targets. His companions squealed with joy, patting and teasing him. His white teeth flashed again in a sheepish grimace.

I felt his blue, blue eyes graze me, then swiftly look back to his task. He was handed another spear. And this one sank into the grass a few feet further than the last. Again, the jostling and bombastic encouragement.

"But he missed," I heard Calanthe say.

Hester opened her mouth to agree, but my father sighed. "Both spears sailed farther than any other bullseye," he said. "The young prince is demonstrating superior skill."

My father's wry tone spoke of his enthusiasm for that idea.

Calanthe smiled as she stared out over the field.

Her expression irked me to no end.

The silly fool is besotted already, I thought.

And you are not? Briar's voice flitted through my mind.

I worked very hard not to frown.

Máel's third shot was beautiful. His spear sailed through the air like a bolt of righteous lightning. Its point embedded itself deeply in the center or the furthest target. Máel leapt onto Cormac's shoulder and raised his fist in the air. His companions cheered and carried him toward the dais, chanting his name.

"Well," my father said, standing and clapping. "It appears the day's contest is done."

The crowd of competitors approached slowly.

I clapped, confused.

"Why, Father?"

"No one will best such a throw. None of my men can, nor his, I expect."

"Any number of my kin could," disagreed Hester, unimpressed.

"That's as may be," my father agreed. "Though none were invited."

She shut her mouth with an audible snap.

My silly sister stood up and leaned against the bannister, clapping wildly. She didn't even know the rules of the game ten minutes before. As the competitors neared with their prince held high, Cormac let him down. Máel approached the dais bare-chested and victorious. The blue ravens tattooed into his collarbone were quite distracting for me.

He grinned at my sister, my father, and then me.

"I've won, My King," he said.

"So you have," agreed my father. "What will you have of me?"

Cormac shouted, "Gold!"

Another answered, "Ale!"

Another, "Your daughter's hand!"

Calanthe tittered like a fifteen-year-old idiot.

But Máel did not look at her.

He was looking at me.

"I'll take only my lady's favor."

The crowd cooed appreciably, every eye straying to me.

I didn't have the first clue what I was supposed to do.

My father jerked me upright by the elbow. "Give him a ribbon from your sleeve."

Befuddled, I plucked the article from my wrist and held it out for Máel's waiting fingers. Our hands touched for that briefest moment, but a slow, steady heat crept up my neck.

His eyes met and held mine.

But he suddenly turned to my sister who pouted pitifully behind her mother. "And my lady Calanthe's first dance, if she'll honor me?"

My sister fairly bounced with glee.

"It will be my honor, my lord."

I hated her then, for the first time.

Truly hated her.

I kept my composure until the men left the field, cheering their prince. When Hester passed me on their way down the steps, she gave me a look of genuine pity.

"I warned you," she whispered, tugging Calanthe away.

Ten

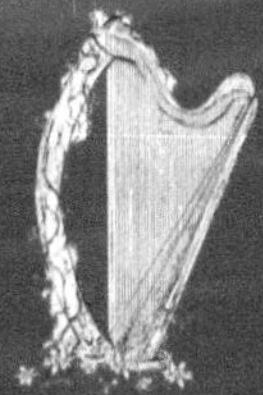

That evening at supper, and all the next day, Máel spent every moment in Calanthe's company. While my newfound appeal worked quite well on lesser lords and their warriors, the High King's brother remained well out of my reach, just as Hester had said he would. He was not there for me. Whatever I imagined had passed between us was nothing more than an eagerness to be polite, and maintain his family's good name. My situation would not be lost on any Eirean nobles. I was the eldest, and should have been married off ages ago. My sister should not have been displayed like this until I had taken vows. But here we were. I must have been an object of no small pity among my father's peers. Especially a prince like Máel.

Of course, I was mortified, but I hid it well.

I'd been hiding it for twenty and two summers, after all.

By midday, after the fighters quit the field and the day's shield contests, I had already grown weary of this farce. My sister was constantly surrounded by a swarm of suitors bowing and scraping from breakfast to supper each day. While I was drawing more attention than ever before, I was no longer the sweet, shy girl of fifteen summers.

I simply couldn't compete.

Even having wished for the beauty of a mad fey king, I was still no match for Calanthe. Máel had eyes only for her. He spent every spare moment by her side. He brought her trinkets, shared her cup at meals, and danced with no one else each night. Mid-week, around the time when steel weapons would be used and these contests become more deadly, I retreated to my rooms.

I'd lost.

So much for my bold declaration.

I opted to do what I should have done from the first, kept to my rooms and waited for everyone to leave. Hopefully, Máel would take my sister with him. And good riddance. If marriage was not to be my future, perhaps my father would allow me to remain at Emain Macha until my cousin came of age and took up the crown. Failing that, maybe a cottage by the sea would not be such a terrible fate?

Having grown bored with the scroll I'd been reading the past two evenings, I shuffled toward the library steps at the center of the royal wing. I had barely hefted my skirts to climb upward, when a hand snaked out of the dark and pulled me up and through the door. It slammed shut behind me.

I drew in a breath to scream.

That same hand clapped over my mouth, holding me close.

I arched my neck to see who had dared, and froze.

Máel smirked down at me, his stubble having become a light beard after days of fighting and horsing around with the men. He had a deep scratch down the side of his face, and bruises lined the part of his throat

I could see in the light of the single brazier beside the door. I shoved against him, but he would not budge.

"Hush now. I will let you loose if you promise not to scream."

I nodded and his hand came away from my face.

"What are you doing here?" I hissed, my eyes narrow.

His usual smile flickered. "I thought you'd be glad to see me. Where have you been?"

I snorted. "Why is my sister's paramour sneaking about looking for me when he could be with his intended?"

"Paramour?" His smile returned with blinding brightness. He still had an arm coiled around my waist. It tightened. "You're jealous!"

I was glad of the poor light, for I felt all the heat in my head rush to my nose. "I am not." I tried to pull away, but he held me closer. "Unhand me."

His eyes glittered in the half-light. "You're maddening, you know. When you came into the hall the other day, I thought I'd murder every man that dared to gawp at you… and here you are, jealous of your little sister."

I jabbed an elbow into his solar plexus and leaped out of reach. I had been my father's favorite, for a time. He taught me where to strike a man when he wouldn't let go.

Surprised, Máel rubbed his ribs. "Ouch."

"I've had enough of this, my lord. You will let me pass and not seek me out again."

But he didn't move. "No, I will not."

"You will, or I will—"

"Marry me."

I stopped.

"What?"

He gave me a lascivious smile that traced my figure from one curve to the next.

"You heard me."

He came closer, palms out like a man soothing a wild mare.

"Deirdre Uí Néill, daughter of Ulaid, be my wife and I will take you far from here."

Although my blood thundered in my ears, I also heard Hester's warning once more.

"No."

He straightened. "What?"

"I said no, now leave me alone!"

I tried to pry past him, but he held me fast.

Suddenly, his face was very near. Our hearts kept pace, beat for beat. His fingers threaded through mine.

I swallowed, turning my chin away.

"No."

"Why not?"

He loosened his grip so I might step back, but did not let go.

"You are here for Calanthe's hand, not mine."

"Áed wishes for Calanthe's hand, not I."

"Yet," my tone iced over, "it is *you* who pays her court, night and day."

"I do so on my brother's behalf. The High King has asked me to press his suit, so I must. Your father understands this and has told me bluntly he intends to refuse him. But it will make little difference. It's either my brother or a Dane, and I think I know which the King of Ulaid would prefer."

"She is besotted with you. You don't discourage her."

He laughed. "She is a maid of fifteen summers. She'd be besotted with a broom if it paid her so much attention."

I said nothing. Showing him only my cheek.

He sighed and removed his hands from my waist.

I made for the door, but he barred the way.

"You think I'm duplicitous?"

"I think actions prove merit, not words. Besides, you don't even know me, nor I you. When you take my sister from here, you will grow bored of her and move on to another. I hoped you might be more. That hope was a weak thing, easily throttled in its cradle."

His brows soared into his hairline.

"You are the most direct woman I've ever met."

"I'm sorry to disappoint you."

"Not at all," he said, with a rue smile. "I like that about you. But you're wrong, I do know you."

It was my turn to laugh. "Now you're reaching."

"It's true. I've been here several times through the years. I trained here every summer until I was seventeen, same as all the other lads in Áed's employ. Ulaid trains the toughest fighters, after all." He leaned close.

"I've seen you many times, actually. Spoken to you once or twice, even. You don't remember me?"

I didn't.

So many warriors came and went under my father's roof it would be impossible to recall them all. Besides, neither my father nor Hester were inclined to introduce their daughters to a gaggle of lads and squires.

"Don't believe me?" he asked, then squinted. "Once, I saw you running through the garden barefooted, your raven braids flying behind you. The next, I saw you asleep in the kitchens, your smock and apron thick with soot, your braids tucked around a fat ginger cat."

I sucked in a traitorous breath.

"Yes, I was only thirteen or so but I was so curious about you. Why would a king let his daughter run wild out of doors and sleep in cinders on a stone floor? Every time I saw you, you were this bright, fey thing, never in the same place twice. Your hair a tangle, face smeared with jam. Then, I stopped seeing you, for years."

He went on, watching my face closely. "When next I saw you, I was twenty and you were a woman grown. Gods, did I suffer then. Do I suffer now." He very gently clasped my hands. Mine were shaking. "You were in here, in your father's library, sat in that window-box over there." He pointed behind me. "It was summer and the window was open. You were reading, your brows drawn in concentration, chewing on your nails."

He stepped closer.

I let him.

"Your hair was down," he whispered, reaching up to touch the unbound part of my braid. "You wore white linen that day, and the sun warmed your cheeks. You were… you are…" He moved closer. "The most startling thing I've ever seen, Deirdre Uí Néill. I begged to come here on my brother's behalf. I had to see you, to speak to you. To know you are real, and not a figment I imagined."

"But— if that is true, why did you not ask my father to introduce us?"

"I have asked your father for your hand, twice. Ask him."

I stared up at him, dumfounded.

"What?"

"He refused me, both times. If you'll have me, I won't hear a third refusal. I will simply take you from here."

My father… *my* father… refused to grant a prince of Eire my hand?

Why?

Why would my father keep me from such a fine match?

It didn't make sense.

None of this made sense.

"You're saying you fancy me?" I asked, incredulous.

"More than that, but yes." He gave a nervous laugh.

"And not my sister?"

"My brother fancies her powerful uncle, frankly, it's a boon that she's comely. But I do not."

I bit my lip.

We stood staring at each other for some time in complete silence. Then, booted feet sounded on the stairs. Voices trailed upward. My father and someone else. They were laughing. My eyes widened in alarm. In a panic, I pulled him deep into the stacks with me, all the way to the far end near the last window. There was barely any light here, just the glow from the brazier by the door and a faint trickle of moonlight through the shutters. I put my hand over his mouth and prayed.

My father came in with Dorcan, a local clansman who'd recently been elected chieftain. They were laughing and clearly in their cups. My father strode to the first stack, showing off his collection of Greek tragedies. He was especially proud of the Latin comedies two stacks over. He'd head there next, and we'd be seen.

Máel cracked the shutters open just a pinch to take a peek outside. It wasn't that far to the ground, perhaps ten or eleven feet. He wasted no time climbing into the window-box and slipping most of himself through the gap in the shutter.

I turned to watch my father and his guest stumble yet closer.

Máel was in position to jump down to the hedges below.

My father moved closer.

"Go!" I mouthed to Máel, nearly apoplectic.

But before he dropped down, he grasped my wrist, pulling me toward him. His mouth claimed mine for mere moments, but it was enough. I believed him. When we separated, the look in his eyes was raw, almost pleading.

I nodded.

With a crooked smile, he slipped into the night.

Shortly after, I was discovered, leaning outside as if to enjoy the air. My father drew up short, confused and slightly cross. I had nearly wrecked the place a few weeks before and had been forbidden to come back, several times, in fact. But I always did. My father didn't mind as much as he let on.

"Daughter?" he slurred, his friend bleary-eyed beside him.

"Father!" I exclaimed, hand to my heart in feigned surprise.

"What are you doin' in here?" he grumbled.

I looked around. "Reading."

He raised a brow and took a look outside. "Mhm. Spying, more like. You'd see more of these fellows, if you bothered to come to meals."

He must have thought I was watching the encampment outside the wall.

I yawned. "Yes, Father. I'll see you in the morning then."

As if I'd never committed a single sin in the whole of my life, I stepped past him and made my way to the door.

He stared after me, suspicion crackling around him.

"Mind you straight to bed! And if I don't see you at breakfast, I'll have you dragged into the hall in your shift."

I curtsied at the door and made my escape.

My heart pounding, I took the steps to my room two at a time.

Eleven

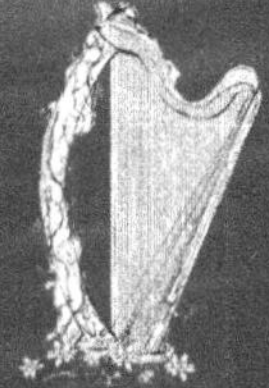

The following week sped by in an eyeblink. I saw Máel at feasts and out on the field during the day. At night, we'd meet in the library. I had never been touched by a man before Máel pulled me into his arms that first night. Though he would not steal my virtue before we were wed, his mouth and hands set fires that would not be quenched. I felt things I could never describe. Happiness, yearning, and fear. Fear that I would lose these feelings, lose him, before my dream was realized. I went to bed every night hollow, aching, and afraid.

The solstice would come and the men would leave.

Where would I be then?

Would Calanthe and I be headed to Tara to wed into the High King's house? Or would it just be me… or just Calanthe?

My mind was a web of conflicting thoughts.

Did he love me?

Did I love him?

Were the flames he kindled in my belly, love?

When he moaned his longing at my nape, his fingers splayed between my thighs, was that love?

I didn't know.

And it drove me mad.

At feasts, he still sat beside my sister, sharing her cup and drawing her smiles like a small sun. And at night, his callused hands roamed my too-warm flesh, his mouth tracing my curves, uncovering secrets I didn't know I bore. In my rooms after, I would relive every moment again and again. An endless loop of pleasure and fear.

Dark smudges haunted my reflection each morning. I could scarcely hold my head up at breakfast. Sometimes I would be far too tired to notice his eyes on me. His subtle smiles. But I was never too tired to see the look on Hester's face. Nor miss the furious cut of her jaw. I'd avoided her successfully for days until she finally cornered me in the garden, plucking rosemary and thyme for Cook.

She wasted no talk on pleasantries.

She knelt so our eyes were level

"Máel has asked for Calanthe's hand."

I knew she would try this, so I tamped down hard on my rising alarm.

"For his brother, Áed, you mean."

Her face twisted into an ugly snarl. "Calanthe has refused. She will have Máel, not his fool brother."

"Whether she will or not, my father will say otherwise. Why are you so disappointed? She will be Queen, just as you hoped."

"Áed will drag your people to ruin. I will not have my daughter burned with the lot."

I set my clippers down and gave her a long look. "What you are speaking now is treason. You mean to subvert the High King as it suits your uncle, not your daughter. Poor Calanthe is just a child and thinks she's in love. That's all she knows."

She curled her lip at me. "Your mating with him won't cheapen Calanthe in the least, only yourself."

"How many times has Máel asked for my hand, Hester?"

She flinched in a way that told me what Máel had said was true.

He had asked, more than once.

He *did* love me.

Was I giddy with happiness because I loved him too or simply because someone wanted me? I tucked that thought away for later reflection.

"He will not have her, Hester. Your uncle must make his peace with Áed."

She jerked to her feet, glaring down at me.

"You poisoned him."

"What?"

"The women are whispering in every corner of the keep. You've used witchcraft to sway him."

"Witchcraft? By what means?"

"Your nose is always buried in those dusty old tomes. You must have learned your spells there."

My mouth swung open but no sound came out.

Technically, she had a point.

I *had* unleashed something in those scrolls, but it wasn't a love potion. Máel had brought his own, it seemed.

She didn't give me a chance to defend myself further.

"I will not allow my daughter to be packed off to Tara to wed a doomed king."

I watched her stalk back to the keep, wondering what my father had said to her.

I decided I should ask.

I found him on the field watching the lists and partway through his third or fourth tankard already. The only thing these men loved more than war games and violence was ale. He brightened more than a sober man would when he saw me.

"Ah! Daughter! Come, watch the bout with me."

I took the seat beside him, careful to avoid his sloshing cup. The men were gathered on the field for the third day of wrestling. I had no idea who was who for the dust and the knot of tangled male flesh gathered at the center. Whoever fought whom, I could not say.

I didn't see Máel, either, which told me he was some-where in that jumble of grunting bodies.

How anyone scored these bouts was mystifying to me.

"Father," I said, keeping my voice low. "I must speak with you."

He spared me a sideways glance that I knew very well.

He didn't like it when women approached him with their problems. My stepmother was meant to handle those issues, so, if I was coming to him now, it could only mean I meant to discuss things with him that I wouldn't or couldn't bring to her. Or it was about her. In either case, my father hated female squabbles and avoided them wholesale.

"What?" he nearly growled.

I looked around us to be sure no one was close enough to hear. "You must give Calanthe to Áed, Father."

"Must I?"

"Hester has as much admitted to me that Ælla means to overthrow the High King and supplant him with his brother."

"Has she?" He stroked his beard.

"She told me she has encouraged Calanthe to reject Áed's suit in hopes Máel might be more amenable to her uncle's claim on the south. But I know that is because while Máel is popular with the men, he does not hold the loyalty of the clans. Ælla hopes to make him a client king."

My father observed me in silence for some time, his tankard forgotten. "And your desire for him would not influence your urgency in the least, I suppose?"

I flushed but held his eye. "He has asked you for my hand, has he not? Does this not give everyone what they want? Áed a wife with strong ties to Ælla of Northumbria, you a daughter who is Queen, Máel a wife with no banners— and you a son-in-law worthy of the crown of Ulaid. Máel would remain here, as your heir, and well out of Ælla's reach. This is the only path you might choose that does not lead to war or more ceded territory."

He sat back, on a huff. "You are so like her, it pains me."

I stiffened. "I am nothing like Hester."

"Not her. Your mother. Aine was a prize in every way, beautiful as a summer's eve, calm as a winter's dawn, and wise as the oldest oak."

My father had never complimented me before.

Nor spoke of my mother to me.

I opened and closed my mouth several times.

"You are right, Daughter. If Máel asks for your hand again, he shall have it."

He tipped his cup at me and before returning it again to his lips, I was gone.

I searched the combat grounds for Máel, but he was not there. His men blinked at me sheepishly, some directly, with lascivious intent. I ignored them and raced from the contest field, relief and joy blossoming in my heart. I ran through the kitchens, the gardens, and the hall. I couldn't find him anywhere.

I looked in the library, the towers, and the palisades.

He was nowhere to be found.

In a last-ditch effort, I ran out to the stables. Twilight had just started to tint the sky a serene violet. The torches had yet to be lit. I walked through the cavernous opening, hearing a soft sound at the back, in the furthest stall. None of the horses seemed bothered by the murmur. They disinterestedly chewed hay at me as I crossed to the rear.

A muffled moan issued from a feminine throat, somewhere ahead. I stopped dead in my tracks, attention drawn toward a poorly lit area. My eyes adjusted, but struggled to make sense of what emerged from the gloom.

In the rear stall, I saw my sister's fair hair spill over her lover's shoulder as he pinned her against the wooden wall. Her skirts were hiked up over her hips, as a man, nude from the waist down, thrust his hips into hers again and again. Calanthe's white leg coiled around his bare buttocks, pressing him deeper as he ground upward, his hands holding her aloft as he traced his mouth over her lips, throat, and bare breast.

I don't know how long I stood there, for I was frozen to the spot, my heart shattering into a thousand pieces. His hips moved faster, harder, his breath coming in rasps.

Calanthe dragged her nails over his buttocks as he moved inside her. "Yes… oh, yes… love," she cried, and spent several moans into his open mouth.

Panting, his back finally stiffened, and he groaned.

He kissed her, mumbling sweet gibberish at her nape.

Just as he'd done with me.

A wave of fury swallowed me then.

I was a fool.

A *fool*.

Just as Hester had said I was.

A half-strangled choking sound escaped my throat. Calanthe's head shot up. She screamed when she saw me and pushed herself free, straightening her dress. Deep red shame pooled in her lovely white cheeks.

Máel turned and paled. Looking from her to me, he tugged his breeches up and reached out a hand. "No, Deirdre. This is not— I can explain."

I didn't care to hear it.

Ignoring him, I stared my sister down.

"I want you to know that he touches me thus every night and has asked father for my hand many times. I want you to know that you are no more special than I, but now twice the slut, for he never took my maiden-head. You deserve each other."

With that, I spun on my heel and took my leave.

Thankfully, I managed to wait till I reached the stairs to fall apart.

Twelve

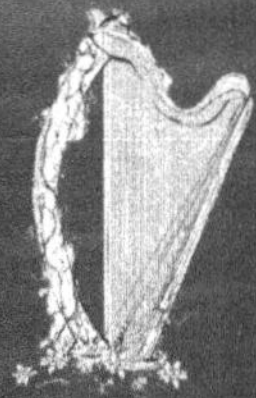

At this point in our story, dear reader, you might pity me. You might think I had been lied to and betrayed, and I had been. But I had also been lying to myself.

Twas I who had dug the knife in, no one else. For I should have known better than to believe a man would want me more than his own ambition. What man would?

I refused to play party to the games downstairs any longer and kept to my room. Cook brought me meals and stroked my hair twice a day, but I would see no one else. Calanthe had tried. Even my father had tried.

I refused everyone. Máel came twice a night, scratching at the door, begging forgiveness.

He would have nothing from me.

Everyone in the keep knew, of course. Probably everyone in Emain Macha.

My hateful stepmother had come upstairs only once, to tell me my father had accepted Máel's troth for my sister's hand. My father couldn't resist once he'd learned what had been going on in the stables. He couldn't sell his daughter to anyone else now that her bridehood had been claimed. Hester had encouraged her, naturally. She had warned me my foolish feelings would come to naught in the end. Calanthe was beautiful and beguiling. Máel was only a man. Beyond this, what man would refuse the opportunity for such an easily claimed crown? His self-love had sunk the lure more deeply than my sister's curves ever could.

Why should it matter to me?

I would dance over broken plates when she'd gone. I'd make offerings to the Morrigan that Máel might pay for his duplicity. I would be glad to see them both gone, forever. But then the tears would come, and I would be overcome with self-pity, disbelief, and rage.

Why did he lie to me?

How could he do that to me?

How could *she*?

Was my life only to be taken in jest?

Why didn't he love me?

Why did he say he loved me only to betray me?

In my darkness, I wished for a return to the point where I believed his lies.

That he loved me.

That he longed for me for years.

That he saw *only* me.

Only me!

Between racking sobs, I asked the gods, the sky, the lough, and the air in my lungs why it couldn't be true? Why could he not see only me? In my heart of hearts, I wished it were true.

And in the shadows of my tower, I failed to hear a bell chime through the sour wealth of my tears.

ON THE LAST DAY OF THE TOURNEY, AT THE HEIGHT OF MID-summer, my father came to my room. His expression loaded with regret, he sat beside me and patted my hands.

"We lost, you and I," he said.

I could only nod.

"Shall we let her win be total?"

I assumed he meant Hester.

"She has everything she hoped for. A prince for her unworthy daughter, revenge on my mother for her memory, and vengeance upon me for existing. Send Ælla my regards, for he will be our new lord soon enough."

My father didn't argue.

He held my hand.

"I am to blame for all of this. When your mother died, I was lost, heartsick. I would have wed a tree if I thought it might give me solace. Of course, she was a design I fell into, rather than a woman I could truly love." His mouth bent into a rue frown.

"I should have never left you to grieve your mother alone. I should never have been blinded by my fair young wife who would ask me to set my child aside in favor of her own. I admit, fearing her uncle's wroth I was spellbound by her, for a time."

"And now?"

"Bitterness and pride, did I not say?" His smile was sad.

"Yours or mine?"

"We are a pair in our failings, it seems."

I sat up and embraced him.

"I'm sorry, Father."

"As am I, Daughter. As am I."

He held me for a bit, stroking my hair.

"I ask again, shall we let her victory be total?"

I knew what he meant.

I sighed.

"No, we shouldn't."

He kissed the top of my head and stood.

"Wear your mother's finest today and no matter what, don't you dare spare either of them a single glance."

I sighed. "It's not really Calanthe's fault, Father. She is as much a pawn in this, as I."

"I know that, and believe she is coming to realize that." He sighed, pausing in the open doorway. "She is a silly, spoilt child who was given every indulgence to keep her mother happy. I hope she can forgive me for that, eventually."

I TOOK MY TIME DRESSING THAT NIGHT, SO I WAS ALONE IN my chamber when Briar appeared in my bronze mirror.

My head whipped around. "You!"

He held his hands up to ward off my glare.

"I told you not to make selfish wishes, didn't I?"

I blew air through my nose at him.

The audacity!

I stared him down, searching for the right words to say to this creature… the author of my sorrows. He'd grown tall, taller than Máel or even my father. His shoulders were wide in his snow-white tunic, and his skin had smoothed out. His hair poured full and shining over his shoulders. Eyes the color of river moss danced over my hair and came to rest on my face.

He made a soft sound I couldn't identify.

Since when had he become so handsome?

While he was not quite as lovely as I'd heard his kind could be, he certainly outshone anyone I'd ever met before.

I hated it.

I hated him.

He had drunk my small happiness down to become this new version of himself.

"You should leave and take this cursed thing with you." I raised my wrist for emphasis.

"I cannot, Deirdre, forgive me." He licked his lips. "If I had had time to consider my debt more carefully, I would have given you anything else. I didn't know it would come to this, I vow it."

His voice, which had once been thin and high as a reed flute, now felt low, close, and rich as velvet. I shivered, despite myself.

"I don't believe you."

His eyes devoured my face so long, I blushed.

"Why are you staring at me like that? Come to crow over what you have wrought."

"It pains me that someone as beautiful, kind, and thoughtful as you would spend your hopes on one so unworthy."

I burst into tears.

He was by my side in a trice, folding my head into the crook of his shoulder.

"I'm sorry," he whispered into my hair. "You seemed so wise that it didn't occur to me how very young you were until it was too late to stop you."

"What should I do now?" I cried, more miserable than I had ever been.

"Come away with me, now."

I lifted my head, sniffling. "I knew it. You mean to steal my life."

He reached out and wiped the tears from my cheeks.

His hand was surprisingly warm.

"I would fill your days with sunlight. I would crush gems from your tears and set stars in your hair. Come with me, Deirdre, and be free of this path."

A strong urge to take his hand washed over me.

But my mind intruded.

My father needed me.

I had made him a promise.

"I can go tomorrow."

He shook his head. "It must be tonight. It must be now."

He cast his eyes down so I might not see what they held.

Dread crept through my veins.

"What do you know?"

Finally, when he spoke, his tone bordered on regret.

"Tomorrow is too late."

I stood, jerking my hands free.

He looked up at me, his expression a plea.

"Deirdre, don't."

Something terrible would happen tonight then.

So be it.

I was in the mood to plague a hundred houses.

Mine, especially.

"I'm going," I said, lifting my skirts and pulling away.

"I won't watch you fail yourself this way," he advised me, his voice firm. "It's not too late to wish for your sister's happiness and scrub this darkness clean. If you choose this path, I can't save you."

Such a dire warning.

It only prodded me to open the door and walk toward my fate.

For good or ill.

Thirteen

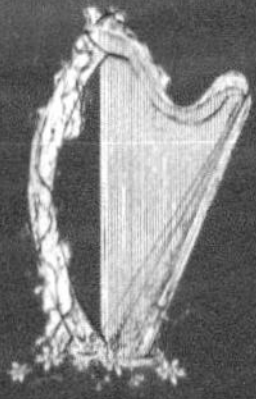

All eyes were on me as I entered the great hall for supper. Every conversation halted. The servants stopped serving. The musicians in the gallery above the dais paused their playing. Out of the corner of my vision, I saw the shape of my sister and her betrothed seated together on my father's left side.

Máel leapt to his feet.

Hester stiffened in indignant disdain.

Calanthe went beet red against her pure white gown.

I noticed much out of the corner of my eye, but I refused to look at any of them. They didn't deserve my attention. Instead, I focused only on my father. His smile bore only pride. Walking forward, I dipped him a curtsy.

"My daughter Deirdre," he acknowledged me, gesturing to the chair on his right side. "Come, sit beside me for the match." I did as I was bid, fully aware of the stares I received from all quarters.

Some spiteful.

Some suspicious.

Some envious.

Curious that the envy should come from Calanthe, who had everything she hoped for. I wore my mother's black gown tonight, with a wine dyed chemise poking through my sleeves and flashing from the divided black linen above when I walked. The bodice was snug, making a pale white valley of my décolletage and enhancing the sharp line of my collarbone. Around my throat I wore my mother's emerald, just a splash of green to catch the light in my eyes. My hair was fully unbound, free to pour over my back and shoulders like a rich, raven-colored cloak. I had dressed for a funeral, knowing the mood suited me best.

The hall had already been cleared for the night's match, the last of the tourney. Since the weather outdoors had soured, the final sword match would be battled out here, in the warmth of our seven braziers. I knew that Máel was to compete against his friend Cormac this night, as the two strongest combatants left. I vowed not to quit the hall before the bout began. The men stared up at the dais, expectantly. Many eyed me with interest. Many with desire. And many more, with pity. I admired the door beyond them and sipped my ale. It was better to remain outwardly aloof, even though my veins screamed fury.

A commotion started somewhere on my left, but I didn't look up. I would not be the one to make a fool of myself here tonight. Calanthe made a frustrated sort of sound. Hester chimed in with a slightly louder command. But Máel must have slipped past my father. As sudden as a shout, he was next to me, clutching the arm of my chair.

"Dierdre," Máel whispered, but the hall echoed the smallest sound, and everyone heard him anyway. "You must let me explain. I didn't mean to—"

I barely had time to set my tankard down before my father launched to his feet, clutched Máel by the throat and slammed him into the tapestry behind us. The Uí

Néill's snarl boomed from every corner of the hall. The men didn't seem to know what to do, nor did I. They stood at attention, uncertain hands on hilts, eyes wide. I spilled out of my chair just in time to avoid being trampled as my father wrestled the smaller man into a full chokehold, lifting his heels from the floor.

Calanthe screamed.

Hester's hand drifted to her own mouth.

The serving women skittered away, screeching.

"How dare you speak to her after what you have done!" Raged my father.

Perhaps I had not said this before, but only the strongest Uí Néill leader can become a King of Ulaid. My father had been a legend in his own time. King Matudán Mac Muirdagh Uí Néill was still the worst possible foe to make. And Máel knew it.

I watched his eyes bulge, his face darken.

"My Lord," he begged. "Please."

"Father," I called out, but he would not hear me.

Calanthe was weeping, her face livid.

My father ignored us all.

"Your mother was my third cousin, you know. When she told me she'd named you for such a mighty king— you, the second son of a second wife, I warned her it would come to no good. You would always want what would never be yours and believe yourself higher than your birthright. Well, tonight, we'll see if I'm right or not."

He let Máel go, who choked and coughed, scratching furiously at his swiftly bruising throat. My father removed his bearskin cloak while Máel gasped to refill his lungs with air. Calanthe attempted to reach him, her mother pulled her back.

My father drew his sword.

"You shall have your final match tonight, Ulaid." He raised his voice so none in the hall could mistake him. "I shall kill Máel Sechnaill, son of Máel Sechnaill, brother to our Ard Ri, Áed Findliath. He has tainted my house with his ambition, and lain hands on that which does not belong to him. Whom shall be his second?"

None spoke up.

Cormac seemed to think it over but eventually shook his head.

"Good," my father said, throwing his sheath down and striding down the dais steps to the center of the hall. "Come then, coward. Come and die."

Calanthe wailed, but her mother held her back by the shoulders. Máel was watching me. I had no idea what to do.

I loved and loathed him all at once.

He had wounded me more deeply than anyone in my life.

But I did not want him to die.

"Deirdre," he croaked. "Forgive me."

I didn't know what to say.

"If you're so sorry, why did you do it? A girl you claimed was only a child. Why?"

"I don't know. I couldn't stop myself."

From the crowd, my father's voice boomed. "COME AND DIE, MÁEL SECHNAILL."

Máel made his way to the steps, but seemed to unable to take his eyes off of me.

"Forgive me… I'll hold the sight of you in the window of my soul all the way to Tech Duinn."

He backed down the stairs, searching my face for any hint of peace. Someone shoved a sword into his hand, but he never looked away. He moved downward, tears spilling into his beard.

"I... I can't." I sobbed.

"I am sorry, Deirdre," he cried. Calanthe screamed behind me. "I lov—" he began, his eyes brimming with sincere tears, but my father's sword cut his exaltation short.

It slammed into Máel's midsection from the left side.

Máel seemed more perplexed by the blow than wounded.

His blue, blue eyes held mine with just a trace of fear.

My father jerked his sword free with a guttural grunt, swung it into his other hand and across Máel's neck from the rear. In utter horror and disbelief, Máel's head wobbled on his bleeding neck, titled right, and toppled to the floor.

Calanthe's screams carried me to the floor beside his corpse, and I saw no more.

I WOKE UP SCREAMING IN THE DARK, REACHING FOR SOME-thing, anything to bring me out.

Cook's hands found me, soothed me.

She whispered that all would be well, over and over, until my breathing evened out.

My father sat at the foot of my bed.

The deep lines of his face seemed etched in stone.

"Father," I said, while Cook fixed me tea at the lar-der. "What did you do?"

He exhaled slowly, his hands shaking on his knees.

"I reacted poorly," he answered, voice trembling.

I swallowed, hard, my ears ringing. "Is he... he is dead?"

"His body was washed and prepared for its journey. It will be returned to his brother at dawn."

The world seemed to whirl past my eyes like a rush-ing river. I collapsed against my mattress with Cook cooing down at me. She placed a wet cloth scented with lavender over my forehead. Somewhere nearby, my father wept.

"Forgive me, Deirdre," he said, summoning an image of Máel walking backward to his death. "I should have wed you to him when first he asked, all those years ago. But you were mine. My most beloved girl. I could not part with you so soon. When next he asked, Calanthe was yet a child, and still I would not let you go." He cleared his throat. "He had barely been here a day when he came again to ask for you, and I again refused him.

"We struck a bargain when he would not leave it be. He would win every contest in the tourney and become my heir, if I would give him your hand."

I stared up at my bed curtains, wondering how I could still breathe with such a sword piercing my heart.

"I considered myself lucky that such a man had been thus faithful to my treasured child." He sniffed. "But Hester had other ideas. She considered this tourney Calanthe's due, owing to her rank, and immediately set about seducing the High King's brother to Ælla's side. I knew it was happening but believed if the lad were truly worthy of you, he would resist your sister's charms and Ælla's promises alike. I suppose... taken together, it would be a man among men who could refuse such a prize."

I said nothing.

My insides were tearing themselves apart.

"In the end, he was the poor second-son of a great king— doomed to live his life in his brother's shadow. I imagine part of him thought to climb to your station, where you might be his without so many trials. I believe he did love you, or at least thought he did. But speaking as a man of royal blood who has made many poor decisions with regard to women, perhaps he was too young to fight the flattery, the charm, and the ambition that coursed through him. A sweet face and a soft lie have parted more men from their honor than any ten swords."

He stood up.

"I am sorry, Daughter. For everything."

I wasn't sure when one or both of them had taken their leave for I was long gone by then.

Deep in dreams that held no sun, only the blue of Máel's eyes begging the forgiveness I would never give.

Fourteen

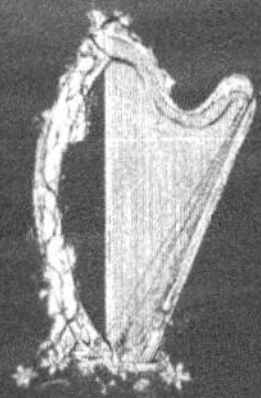

Calanthe woke me. I didn't know what hour it was nor how long I'd been asleep. She held a knife to my throat.

"He chose you," she blubbered, pressing down until the blade bit into my flesh. I started, hand flying to the hilt. She slapped my hand away then struck either side of my face before pressing down harder still.

"Cal…an…the," I gasped. "Why?"

"Why?" She shrieked in my ear, her eyes wild. "You *dare* ask me why? You stole him from me. He's dead now, because of you. Because father loves you more than me. Because Máel loved you more than me. Because *everyone* loves you more than me."

She broke down into racking, rib-cracking sobs.

I stared up at her, confused.

"In which magical otherworld do you live where *I* am the favored sister?" I asked, not caring if she cut my throat. "You've been given absolutely everything you wanted from the moment you were born till now. Dolls, toys, dresses, baubles, songs, gifts… you've been spoilt bloody rotten every single day you have lived beneath this roof."

Her hand shook on the dagger's hilt.

She loosened the pressure, and I slowly sat up, never taking my eyes from her tear-streaked, bloated face.

"In what world have I taken absolutely anything from *you*, Calanthe? I have been nothing but the regrettable shadow of a woman long dead. Tell me, sister. What have I taken from *you*?"

I swatted her blade away and she covered her eyes.

"You had the best gowns, a gaggle of maids, the best food, the best room, the best seat at table. You had the admiration of everyone around you from the servants to visiting lords and dignitaries. They call you 'the fairest maid in Ulaid' and strew flowers everywhere your delicate feet might walk… and you have the gall to accuse me of taking something from *you*?"

She heaved a horrible moan, curling in on herself.

"You're not wise, brilliant, gifted, or even particularly kind. You struggle with letters I learned as a toddler and shun anyone your mother tells you is beneath you. You walk through this palace everyday like you swallowed the sun whole and you're not even smart enough to know how incredibly stupid, vain, and infuriating you really are.

"And you just had to have him," I went on, beyond concern for anything but making her feel as terrible as I did. "Was it your mother's idea or yours to spread your legs to tempt him away? Huh, Calanthe? Whose idea was it?"

She held up her hands. "I *loved* him, Deirdre."

"You barely knew him, Cal," I sneered. "It took you less than a moon to throw your virtue at the only man who didn't want you, just so you could win. Isn't that right? Or will you lie to me as easily as you lie to yourself?"

She wiped her face on her sleeve, working to compose herself. "He came to me one day, to tell me that his brother had offered more for my hand than Ælla could promise. He said he didn't need Ælla's leavings, vowing to stand by his brother. He said if I didn't wish to wed Áed, then he would leave me be and let my father sort it out. But," she covered her face again, "I struck him. I called him a coward and a fool. Then, I kissed him, and next thing I knew, we were both in the hay. That first time… it just happened. He cursed me, cursed himself, and left. But it happened again and again. Before the last time, when you… saw us, he claimed he was leaving, begging me to accept Áed's troth. I just wanted *him*," she wailed. "I would do anything he asked, so long as he stayed with me."

I absorbed everything she said with equal parts hatred and pity. Máel, lovely, strong, charming Máel.

He was a shite, all told.

I ached for him nearly as much as I ached to drag him from his grave and kill him again. But Calanthe was not innocent either.

She wanted him because I wanted him. Given how easy it was for her to take everything else from me, she couldn't abide losing to me. Not even once. I saw her as clearly as I could see myself in my bronze mirror. She was just as jealous of me as I was of her, perhaps more so. I had nothing left to prove.

"Why did you come here tonight?" I asked her.

She stood up and for the first time, I noticed her hair had been shorn. It swung around her jaw in choppy, irregular blonde waves. I must have made some sound, for she reached into her valise to produce her heavy gold braid.

"My mother… the women… they say you used magic to call him to you."

I went cold. "What?"

"I-I thought," she hiccupped, "if you had such gifts, you could, you might… call him back."

A star exploded in my head.

"*What did you just say?*"

She clasped her hands together and knelt before me.

"Please, Deirdre. I'll give you anything you want. All my most precious things." She held up her hair like an offering. Without it, she looked like any other young girl, her face round with the swell of youth. "Please, Deirdre!"

I hated her more than I have ever hated anyone.

More than Hester.

More than my father.

More than Máel.

More than myself.

In that moment, I wished that either one of us would just vanish. Deep down, I hoped it would be me.

I never wanted to see her again.

"Leave," I said. "You are no sister of mine."

She got up and fled the room in a fit of tears, leaving her sad golden braid behind. It wasn't until much later, when I'd calmed down, that I noticed my bell and its chain were gone.

Dawn cracked cold and gray through my shutters. A newfound chill crept through the gaps, dusting my nose and cheeks with frost. My fire must have gone out in the night and it seemed autumn was already scratching at my window.

I got up, feeling every inch the worst I'd ever felt.

My eyes were so swollen I had trouble blinking, and my throat felt as though I'd swallowed fire. I winced when I got up, every muscle protesting as I carefully made my way to my mirror. My eyes were two dark pits in a ghostly thin mask. My hair hung in limp, oily ten-drils, my lips were pale as cream. At my throat, Calan-the had left an angry red line that had dribbled blood onto my collar. I glanced at her braid coiled on the furs at my feet and quickly looked away. I thought about changing my dress but decided I didn't give a damn what anyone thought of me today.

I made my way downstairs, but didn't see anyone in the hall for the first time that month.

I went to the kitchen next.

No one was there, either.

Where had everyone gone?

Like an unholy spirit, I drifted from chamber to chamber, looking for anyone, everyone. I must have wandered about for half an hour or more before I heard the keening from the courtyard. Shambling through the great hall, I shuffled outside to the railing and looked down. The whole castle was there milling back and forth beneath the portcullis. The women were all weep-ing into their aprons.

What now? I thought, swiftly numbing to tragedy.

Hester's shrill screams rent the air beyond the keep.

I knew it was her for the smattering of Norse oaths commingled with Eirean curses.

I drifted to the wall.

The wailing grew to such a pitch that my skin tingled.

What has happened?

I saw Cook leaning over a cart, weeping into her hands. Hester was a puddle of fabric and mussed hair on the other side, keening into a pair of still legs beneath a white dress.

The figure in the cart had no shoes on.

All the air was wicked out of my lungs on a single breath, as if something had struck me in my guts. Without thought, I raced downstairs into the courtyard and sped under the portcullis to the cart. My father knelt at the gate, hunched over. Heads turned as I approached. Their faces cinched when they saw me. One of the serving women made the sign against evil. Another hissed at me.

What is happening?!

I passed my father and headed for the cart.

"No, Deirdre!" he called after me. "Don't look."

Cook saw me and threw herself from the cart to stall me.

"No, my lady! No!"

But it was too late.

I saw who lay there, milky eyes staring up at the sky.

Her dress was soaked through, marred by moss and mud. One of her breasts was exposed and half-eaten by crabs or eels. The tip of her nose had been bitten off, and she'd lost a chunk from her beautiful cheek. As I got closer, I could see she had lost one of her eyes, too, and her left earlobe. Her fingers and lips were blue-black, her flesh pale as a fish's belly.

Someone made a guttural, unnatural scream.

A sound for lost souls on windswept moors or nightmares lurking in garden pools. I don't know how long it took for me to realize the sound came from me. Cook caught me against her, my body heaving.

I had just seen her!

We had just spoken!

She came to me… and I…

You wished for her to disappear.

Calanthe, my sister, my rival, my only friend, my worst enemy, lay in that cart. She had flower petals in the short remnants of her hair. Gone.

Gone.

Gone.

My keening seemed to pierce the haze. Hester lifted her head and spilled out of the cart spitting with rage. She leapt at me but one of my father's men caught her round the waist.

"YOU DID THIS!" she cried. "You killed my girl! You murdered your sister!"

My father was suddenly there, prying her out of the guards' arms. "Love, she drowned herself. These fishermen saw her go into the water and not come up. They spent the whole night looking for her."

Hester's face distorted so much, she might have sprouted fangs. The whites of her eyes consumed her irises. Her finger came up, shaking but imperious. "Because she's a WITCH!"

She paused to howl, half-collapse into my father's arms, and then launch upright again in an attempt to claw herself free. In her struggle to get at me, she struck her own nose and blood soon dribbled onto her dressing gown. She looked terrifying.

"She bewitched my girl after she bewitched Lord Sechnaill. You ALL KNOW it to be true!"

I recoiled from her ravings and looked around. Besides Cook and my father, most of the folk gathered appeared to agree with her. Several women tucked their thumbs into their palms and spat in the dirt at my feet.

I lurched backward. "Stop it!"

Hester fought free of my father and threw herself at me, drawing her nails across my cheek. The hot sting wrenched a cry from my mouth.

Hester spat blood into my face.

"Die, WITCH!"

My father jerked her up by the collar and passed her to his guards. "See that she gets to our rooms and have her women draw her a bath."

Her screeching lunacy circled the courtyard. "Kill the WITCH!" she repeated with all her strength. "KILL HER! SHE CURSES US ALL!"

My father then turned as if to give me a hand up, but a stone sailed out of the crowd and struck me in the head.

Light exploded behind my eyes.

Something warm tracked over my brow.

I lay inert on the damp, muddy road, neither up nor down, awake or asleep. I don't know how long I was there, but when I snapped to, my father's guards stood over me with their swords high.

"Get her out of here!"

Someone shouted to someone who then scooped me up like a broken doll and ran inside with me over his shoulder. Through a bleeding-red haze, I watched the incensed crowd attack my father at the gates of his own castle.

Frigid fear settled over my bones.

The people believed what Hester accused me of.

They believed I was a witch.

Perhaps they were right.

COOK LED ME TO MY ROOM AND TOLD ME TO PACK MY things quick as I could. Unsteady on my feet, I felt around for whatever I could, although I was confused about what I was looking for. I had a hard time focusing, and my eyes were full of blood.

I fell to the rug with a startled thump.

Cook knelt beside me. "No, my lady. No! Your step-mam has done for you this time. The folk believe her, you see, and there's nothing to stop them now… not even your father. They'll burn the house down to get you out of Emain Macha. The Others bring bad luck, and they think you've been touched."

I broke down weeping, blood dribbling on the floor.

They were right.

I *was* fey-touched.

I *was* doomed.

And I had doomed Máel.

And Calanthe.

And now my father.

He burst into my room just as I thought of him.

Eyes wild, he was bleeding from one arm.

"Get her gone!" he said, moving to help me from the floor. He took off his own heavy cloak and slung it over my shoulders. "You must leave now, Deirdre, or I can't save you."

He embraced me, held me tight to him for several breaths.

"This is my fault. *All of this* is my fault. I should never have held the tourney. I should have wed you to Máel when he first asked for your hand. Before that, I should never have brought that woman here. But it's too late now. They will force me to give you up if you don't leave."

I thought of Briar.

All of this started with the scroll.

A scroll I had unwound with my own hands.

A gift I never wanted but still used.

A curse I brought down on myself.

On all of us.

I wanted to die.

But I was out of wishes.

My father wiped blood from my face and handed me a large sack. "This contains your mother's jewels and all the coins I could gather. Take them, and don't look back. I'm sorry. I love you, Deirdre."

Then he was gone. From the roar of the crowd gathering outside, he had his work cut out for him.

Those people want you dead, I told myself.

And you deserve to die.

Cook wasted no time. She took the clippers from the larder and hacked off my hair, stuffing it into the sack my father had given me. "You can fetch a fine price for this, in the north," she said.

My sister's braid glittered on the ground beside me. I snatched it up and shoved it into my apron before Cook saw.

It wouldn't do for my last ally to see just how guilty I really was. Before I knew it, we were out in the hall and down the back stairs to the kitchen garden. If anyone saw, they didn't try to stop us. We ran from the outer wall into the center of town, then past that to a peddler Cook knew with a wagon. By evening, we sat in the back of that wagon being driven as far north as the fellow would carry us. At noon the next day, we reached a small hamlet and hired another.

Two days later, we came to a seaside town on the rim of a great wilderness.

This is where Deirdre Uí Néill's story comes to an end.

And Ciara's story begins.

Fifteen

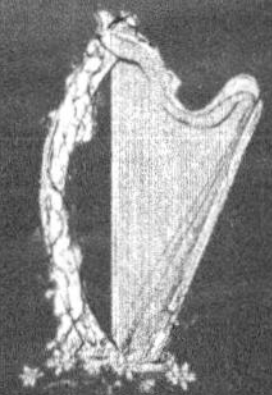

I lived in a cottage, in a wood, a stone's throw from the sea. I hung herbs over my door in the summer and furs along the walls each winter. I had a small garden that fed me through the year, a tiny cellar out back where I kept my stores. I kept my loom under the window facing my flower patch, so I might enjoy my roses in the warm months. I had a stone hearth with a fine black griddle for cooking, a porcelain kettle I'd traded seven kerchiefs for, an oak wardrobe filled with comfortable homespun, a stone wash basin built into a pine larder below many shelves stacked with wooden bowls and iron pots, and up a sturdy ladder, a sleeping loft with my bed and a fine oak wardrobe I'd bought from the haberdasher in town.

Cook's bed had lain across from mine for many years. Without her, I'd no doubt have died that very first winter. She taught me to cook, clean, grow food, prepare stores, build a fire, properly empty a chamber pot, shear sheep, spin wool, make yarn, care for my animals, curdle cheese, bargain for household goods, and how to keep myself busy to pass the time.

She taught me how to live.

She took my mother's jewels and bought this house, our pony Nell, a fat cow named Gert, and a half dozen sheep. She sold my hair for my loom, and planted the very roses under which I'd eventually bury her.

I wept for years after she passed, more alone than ever I had been, acutely aware that I never told her how much I loved her. Around five years or so after we'd arrived, we had gone into town to sell our scarves and stoles for the coming winter. A dread fever had taken root among the townsfolk. Before we arrived home that evening, we were both afflicted.

Cook died four days later.

I had nearly joined her.

If it weren't for Briar, I surely would have.

I didn't like to be grateful to him, being that he was a frequent uninvited guest that I loathed with my whole soul. But he did save my life that time. Well, if I were honest, it was probably much more than the one time. I never chopped my own wood, you see. Nor struggled to find seeds to plant each spring. Nor did my animals ever sicken or die before their time. I know I owed these blessings to Briar, but I didn't care.

I refused to see him.

Refused to speak to him.

Refused to hear him.

He would watch me from the trees behind the house while I worked at my loom, his face bearing immeasurable sorrow.

I ignored him.

I would often feel him standing at the window some nights, looking up at my sleeping loft. I would pretend he wasn't there.

When my animals were mysteriously fed some mornings, my clippers would turn up exactly where I'd misplaced them, when holes in my shoes disappeared, when my bathwater kept warm for a full hour, when my tea never chilled, when my pony never needed shoeing, and my flowers bloomed in every season— I knew Briar was with me.

And still, I hated him.

Fifteen years from the day I'd fled Emain Macha with Cook in the back of that wagon, I hadn't uttered a single word to him, no matter how often he visited me. I would catch sight of him several times a week, but each time, I would bend my head to other tasks.

He did not deserve my attention.

Because of him, my family was dead.

Because of him, my home, my status, and my good name had been stripped from me. Because of him, I was a thirty-seven-year-old spinster living at the arse-end of the world, alone. Because of him, the townsfolk treated me coolly, an outsider who'd arrived in the dark of night with one companion and a bag full of gems. A strange hermit who only came to town to sell her needlepoint or make a trade. An odd, reclusive woman who spoke with a low-country accent and bore a suspiciously courtly manner.

I'd never assimilated into their town for fear of anyone learning the truth of my origins. It was better that they nodded to me in passing, brought me their dresses and quilts to mend, or merely purchased my shawls on market days. The fewer people I engaged with, the fewer I would need to lie to.

While it was common practice in the far north of Ulaid to keep one's eyes on one's business, this didn't mean that one such as I would be expressly welcomed, either. The Others were a particular menace outside of the major settlements, thus no one wanted to invite the misfortune they spread… even here, where most who were 'touched' were eventually sent.

If they weren't killed.

As I'd learned the day Cook spirited me out of the keep, people did terrible things when they were afraid. While the folk around here might not burn me, as my stepmother and her followers meant to— I would be driven out, at the very least. I'd rather the townsfolk here believe I was an aging spinster who'd been in the way of a new marriage. Or a recalcitrant daughter who'd gotten with child young and was sent away. Or best of all, a widow who refused to marry again. The last was the ideal option, given that I'd lose no respect in anyone's mind. In any case, I kept to myself, avoiding Briar's ceaseless attempts to make amends with me and any wagging tongues I could thwart along the way.

I projected the air of a widow who was happiest alone, and introduced myself as Ciara Ap Muir when asked.

In the many years I'd been in this cottage, several men had made plain their interest, but I rebuked all comers. Even the washerwomen and barmaids that attempted to get to know me, soon discovered I was a stone without a seam. One couldn't draw anything out of me, even when Cook had died and I became ravenous for company of any sort. Now, when I hitched my small wagonload of goods to Nell and headed into town for business, I could have a tankard of ale at the tavern or stop and chat with various shopkeepers without them asking me probing questions. People knew me, knew my pony and my goods. They would wave, smile, and sometimes stop to exchange pleasantries. But that was all.

No one invited me into their lives.

Nor did I invite them into mine.

We existed side-by-side.

Separate and content.

All save for one person, that is.

A man named MacTierney, a successful merchant from town, had a son named Breccan who fancied himself a bard. When the lad was perhaps ten summers or so, he'd fallen into the stream behind my house and nearly drowned. Had I not been washing my linens at that precise moment, he would have. Growing up on Lough Neagh as a half-wild child, my father used to jest that my mother had been a seal. Good thing for Breccan, I could swim for both of us.

Thereafter, he drifted past my door at least once a week to show off a shiny new pebble he'd found, a pelt from his first rabbit, his first black eye, and his first whisker when his voice changed. The lad became a regular visitor, and in his case, I did not mind a whit. His mother passed before my coming, and his father had wed again.

He and the woman did not get on.

Naturally, I'd developed a soft spot for him. I got in the habit of setting an extra place for him at supper, if he happened by. He did more often than not. I laid out fresh trousers, tunics, and belts for him every autumn. He'd wear them until they ran threadbare, and eventually, I'd replace them. Perhaps I was less a surrogate mother for him than he was a son to me. As he got older and girls became more interesting than a strange widow in the woods, I saw less of him. I would still see him at Imbolc and Beltane when the town gathered to trade and swap tales of faraway lands. By this point, Breccan's father had already tossed the lad out on his ear for picking up the harp rather than the pestle. From what I'd heard about town, he'd been staying with the baker and her daughters for nearly a year.

I still raised my eyebrows at that.

But, of course, I did not pry.

Young people must be free to make their own mistakes.

Hadn't I learned as much myself ages ago?

When I grew nostalgic, Briar would sigh from somewhere nearby.

I would never turn around.

Breccan hadn't been to see me in some time when he ambled up my walk one morning. I was busy sweeping the porch when I spied his ginger head bobbing down the hill. His freckled face lit up when he saw me.

He waved, all limbs and elbows at nigh-on twenty years old.

"Ciara," he cried, running over to embrace me, his harp bouncing on his back. I didn't like to be touched as a general rule, but Breccan was family by now.

I hugged him back and wrinkled my nose. "You smell like burnt turnip tips."

He pulled away, sniffed at his jacket, and made a face. "Oh, aye, I do. Sorry about that. Been walking for miles."

I sighed in exasperation. "Did you happen by because you knew I had fresh tunics made for Beltane?"

He dimpled in perfect innocence. "You wound me, Ciara, deeply."

I sucked my teeth at him and took the offensive jacket to hang out on the line. "There's fresh shirts for you in that bundle on the mantle," I said, jabbing clothespins into the corded wool collar.

I'd made the jacket for him too, along with nearly every shirt he'd worn since he was sixteen summers old. He wouldn't wear anything else. He squealed with delight to discover I'd made him two very fine flax tunics, one actually dyed a rich green from my own mugwort and thyme. He came out again and kissed my cheek, rushing off to the river with my soap.

"Don't lose it this time!" I shouted after him, shaking my head.

I was already working on supper by the time he returned, wet-haired, clean, and wearing his new green shirt. "Ciara!" he said, barely containing the excitement on his face. "The most wonderful news!"

"Well, go on then," I mumbled, tasting the stew I was reheating. "I'm all ears."

He flopped onto a stool while I worked over the hearth, gesticulating excitedly.

"The King's wedding!"

"Mmm." I smiled patiently.

"The Ard Ri's daughter will wed the King of Ulaid at Beltane!"

Sixteen

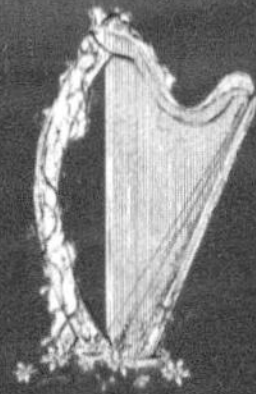

It was not uncommon for villagers and simple townsfolk to discuss the ruling class, and particularly the ruling Uí Néill Clan and its king. My father had died of a fever not a year after Cook and I took up residence here, and Hester had remarried some minor southern chieftain not long after. In Ulaid, only the strongest could be king— but the men of my family had been hailed the strongest going back to the mighty Fergus Mac Léti.

My cousin Lethlobar was the natural choice, but he had to win many trials and then be elected by men to lead them. All told, it took Lethlobar nine moons to win the Kingship of Ulaid. Now, he had ruled for nearly fourteen unmemorable summers, and given his poor health, his son Niall Noígíallach had been elected to take his crown. With a royal wife such as Áed's granddaughter Roana at his side, he might become a greater king than even my father had been. I kept my face neutral while I ladled hot stew into Breccan's bowl.

"That's wonderful, dear," I mused.

One could not escape one's past entirely, no matter what the storybooks say. I was reminded of my former life often.

I didn't love it, but there we are.

"Is that not the best news you've ever heard? We shall have a proper queen in Ulaid. All the girls are tittering over what she might look like, what fashions she might favor. It's the talk of the north." He got out around mouthfuls of stewed cod and leeks.

Taking my own seat, I chewed with a raised brow.

Squinting at me, he laughed. "You're never amused by tales of the fine folk down south, though everyone in town says you used to be one of them."

I worked very hard not to react.

"People in town say lots of things, laddie. For one, that you've promised your troth to two of the baker's daughters, and one in the next town five miles away." I took another bite and pointed my spoon at him.

He went about a dozen shades of red, which told me the tales were likely true, and squirmed in his seat. "They don't speak of you with disrespect, Ciara. Everyone knows your husband died. Even my stepmam says it takes guts to do the honorable thing."

A flash of Máel's bright blue eyes struck me then.

His head tilting forward, then tumbling to the floor.

I shoved the memory deep and forced a mild smile.

"That's fine praise, from your stepmam, that."

He chewed noisily, a habit I'd never been able to cure, cocking his head at me. "Why didn't you remarry," he asked for the first time, perhaps ever.

"I'm sure I don't know what you mean."

"Well, you're still… erm, handsome enough. Many men round town had thought to ask, if you were inclined."

"Eat your stew."

He dipped his spoon, a mischievous sparkle in his brown eyes. "I thought you were a water sprite when we first met. Herne, was I smitten. You were very— erm, you know."

I rolled my eyes.

"You were saying, about the King of Ulaid's wedding?"

I forbade him to polish his charm on me in his youth, but every now and then, he tried anyway.

He laughed, wiping his mouth. "Ah, yes! The Uí Néill has summoned all the bards of Ulaid to play at his wedding feast."

His excitement burned from his cheeks.

I blinked back at him for some time.

"And you'll go?"

"Of course! And I was hoping." He coughed, looking down sheepishly. "We might travel together."

I said nothing for quite a while, eventually getting up to set my empty bowl on the larder beside my stone wash basin. I leaned into it a bit, revisiting ghosts through a blank wall, my back to him. "Why would you ask me to join you?"

"Well..." He cleared his throat. "The Beltane market has been canceled this year so all of our merchants can sell their wares at the event. Even my father and his wife are going. Everyone knows they will earn thrice more than a yearly sum in a single week."

My blood chilled.

I was counting on the Beltane market as I had every year I'd been here. I wouldn't make it through the winter without the funds I raised there. And he knew that, which is why he'd come. I turned and something in my face made him get up.

"Oh no! Ciara, did you not know about Beltane?"

"No, I didn't."

"I'm so sorry! I thought Alla or Tomlin would have said."

"I haven't been to town this month."

He scrubbed his hands over his face. "Well, I'm glad I came then. Caravans leave in a fortnight. I can help you load your wagon."

I was speechless.

This was not at all what I had expected him to come and tell me. Usually, he came to fill my ear with town gossip, meaningless squabbles, or anything he found remotely interesting. I hadn't known he'd come to seal my fate in just a few sentences. Without the Beltane market, I or my animals might starve.

I had no choice.

My guts twisted, my hands shook.

My breath came in ragged gasps.

I saw Máel's head tilt at that unnatural angle again. My sister's remaining eye, staring blankly up at nothing, half of her face eaten away. I saw my father's horrified, heartbroken expression. I saw the crowd gather around me, hissing and making signs against evil.

Breccan came up behind me, setting a cautious hand on my shoulder. "Ciara." He prodded, gently. "What happened to you there?"

I think I opened my mouth to answer him, but a dizzying darkness slowly crawled into my eyes.

Soon, I saw no more.

WHEN I AWOKE, I WAS STREWN ACROSS MY SMALL SETTEE beside the hearth, a cool cloth on my forehead. I heard Breccan rattling around, attempting to do the washup after his meal. He'd never mastered the task, and my crockery was half-scrubbed and stacked haphazardly on the larder to dry.

He beamed when he saw me. "Ciara!" He raced over, patting my hands. "You scairt me to the Otherworld and back just now."

"Mmm," I grunted noncommittally, rubbing my temple. "Forgive me, I haven't been sleeping well," I lied. The weather had taken a rather warm turn this season, but Breccan wasn't stupid.

His expression said he knew better, but he nodded agreeably. "It *has* been unbearably hot for some weeks."

I hummed commiseration and sat up.

"I don't know if I'm well enough to travel."

He looked to my worktable covered in yarn, rolls of stacked shawls, and fine linen tunics tied in bundles as his had been. "How much did all of that cost?"

My answering sigh was bone deep.

"I thought so," he said. "You might be able to convince Mara Rooney to sell some for you, just you know she'll knick as much as she trades."

"Do you think I could sell them to your father, maybe, beforehand?"

He shook his head. "Doubtful. He's spent all of this year's savings already gearing up for Beltane. Now with this, he'd never earn it back. Everyone who can is going. Those who don't might have a hard year."

A bitter knot of dread twisted my throat.

I was one of them.

I had had a good Imbolc and bought more wool at market than I'd brought to trade. If I didn't go, I wouldn't be able to feed the animals I depended on for my own wool and sustenance. I could probably eke by with my limited stores, but my sheep would certainly starve, and my business would die.

'Ere I starved this winter or next, it didn't matter.

I had no choice but to go.

Though I struggled with it for many minutes, trying to glimpse a way out of this mess, I could spy no escape.

"I worry about you, up here all alone. I worry as much as if you were me own mam, if you don't mind me saying as much. Would break my heart to know you could faint like that and no one here to catch you."

I groaned, expelling every bit of air I possessed.

I was soundly beaten, and we both knew it.

"How soon must I be ready," I asked him finally, as one asked an executioner which blade he would use to dispatch them.

"A sennight," he replied, his brown eyes apologetic.

I felt bad about it. It was hardly his fault his happy news had caused me such distress. How could he have known?

"I will help you get loaded and my father has said your flock will be safe in his field while we are away."

Well, Breccan seemed to have thought of everything.

I supposed that was it then.

I was going home.

Later that night, when Breccan had gone, I sat up in bed, worrying at my nails. What if I were recognized?

While it was true that I'd changed a great deal in fifteen summers, surely I was still the same person, with the same face?

I pressed a hand to my cheek, feeling the faint lines time had carved into the corners of my eyes, in hints around my mouth and throat. I ran my fingers through my hair now shot through with silver. I didn't have to touch my arms and bosom to know that much of my well-fed frame had melted over hard seasons and a limited diet. I was not the same person. Maybe they would *not* see the king's mad daughter, after all. Maybe they'd simply see an aging matron selling yarn and shawls in the courtyard stalls, as I'd seen so many in my youth.

I sat there for a while, wrestling anxiety before I could stand it no longer. I got out of bed, wrapped a shawl around my shift, and stepped into my shoes. The night air was heavy with humidity and the promise of rain, but I shivered anyway. I picked my way around the house to sit in the grass before Cook's roses, tucking my shawl around my knees.

What would Cook say, if she knew what I was about to do?

Would she approve or warn me away?

I didn't think I had much choice.

No other brilliant ideas sprang to mind, either.

A shadow crossed the moon and I looked up. If Briar had been handsome before that fateful day a lifetime ago, he was breathtaking now. His silver-blond hair spilled over his shoulders to his narrow belt, fine and gleaming as any spiderweb in a sunbeam. His eyes, which had once seemed so captivating, now sucked an unconscious breath from my throat. Their arresting green wasn't merely the color of river moss, but rather the color of river moss at every point in the day, endlessly shifting from dawn to midnight. Those magnetic, ever changeable pools, watched me solemnly from the fenceline. His skin was a shade between sunshine and moonglow pulled taught over impossibly fine bones with a brow that would make a woman weep. He was taller than any man I'd ever seen, even my father, and his shoulders wider. In his fine white tunic and breeches, he might have been carved of marble.

"Dierdre," he called me, a name I'd nearly forgotten.

His voice was like the smallest dusting of wind at your nape but as deep as a river pouring over a canyon of ageless stone.

An unbidden chill traced over my skin.

"At last, you seek me."

I gave him my cheek, heart racing, despite myself. Had I really not looked at him in all these years? "I realized," I struggled to keep my voice even, "I have no one else to turn to for advice."

He raised a brow that made my insides twist. "You'd ask *me* for my opinion?"

I exhaled through my nose, pulling my shawl close. "Don't play coy. Since you clearly won't leave, you must know what's going on."

He stepped forward with a deep frown. "I do."

"What would you do, if you were me?"

He considered me in silence for some time. "Are you asking me because you believe you have no choice, or because you want someone to choose for you?"

"I'm asking what *you* would do in my place."

He looked around at my small garden, the rear of the cottage, and the trees over the ridge. "You are… content here?" he asked.

"Did I have a choice but to be otherwise?"

He shifted where he stood, crossing his arms.

"Deirdre, you had many choices, but refused to see them."

My nostrils flared and I chewed my lower lip.

He wasn't wrong.

I blamed him, loathed him, really— but in truth, he'd attempted to return a kindness by giving me a gift. A gift I'd been too young and self-centered to value. He'd had almost no say in what I'd used that power for and had cautioned my choices at every turn. I might be angry with him till I died, but my fate wasn't really his fault.

It was mine.

I'd made selfish choices mired in petty thoughts and feelings. And I had paid for them. While I could acknowledge my own failings at this point in my life, it didn't mean I wanted to be scolded for them.

"Will you help, or should you leave?"

He came closer. "I have never gone, have I?"

No, he hadn't.

"Why have you kept coming?" I'd been meaning to ask for years.

He managed to look uncomfortable. "You haven't made it easy, I'll admit."

"Answer the question."

He inched even closer. He smelled like pine needles in a snowbank. Or fresh cut wheat in an oncoming rainstorm. My nose twitched. His nearness made my ears buzz.

I had to crane my neck to look up at him.

"I owe you," he said softly, his expression full of something else… something unknowable. I flushed. "But that is only a half-truth."

"What's the other half?"

He stepped so close, his hair brushed my collarbone.

"When the time is right, you'll know."

As if a spell had been broken, I recoiled and moved back a few paces. The disappointment on his face was obvious.

It made me angry.

"Do you know how to answer a direct question?"

"When you are ready for answers, I'll tell you anything you wish to know."

I threw up my hands and stomped back toward the house, muttering under my breath.

"Deirdre." His beautiful, too warm, too perfect voice turned me back around. "If you wish to keep your life as it is, this will cost you several hard winters… but you'll survive it."

"And if I go?"

He said nothing for a long while, just watched me sadly.

When at last he spoke, I felt like he only repeated what I already understood.

"Other choices must be made."

I nodded once.

"Damned if I do, damned if I don't." I laughed, bitterly. "Fine. I'm going, then."

Before I closed the door on him, he asked, "Will you speak with me again?"

Was it merely guilt that drove him?

I didn't know.

"Maybe," I replied, locking the door before I climbed up to bed, willing my screaming heart to silence.

THE FIRST FEW NIGHTS, I SPENT WEAVING AND DARNING like never before, determined to inventory enough wares for the massive market. I tried not to dwell on how surreal it all felt. My father had been the king, after all. My family was the most powerful in the North… and here I was, a common merchant. Still, a far preferable fate to the one I'd have endured had I stayed. Rather than dwell on things I could not change, I kept my mind on my labors and allowed Breccan to find a wagon and make arrangements for my animals.

I would miss Gert and my flock dearly, but I'd elected to leave them behind lest something happened to me. I forced myself to plan without dwelling on my feelings. I even set up a small nest egg for Breccan, including a tiny handful of coins that I'd managed to set aside every year. I also made a deal with his father that Breccan was to inherit my cottage, to which he grumpily acceded after a lengthy diatribe regarding the boy's 'failings.' Breccan's father and I never saw eye to eye on that score, but in the end, I had my way. Who else did I have but Breccan? I fervently hoped to return home and die within these four walls, but if I didn't, at least someone would have a home and hearth. Who knew? Maybe it might encourage the boy to calm down and finally take one of those girls to wife?

Traveling through Ulaid, even in late summer,was always a risky prospect, especially when your caravan consisted of merchants coming south with mounds of wares and copious lockboxes filled with coins. Brigands were a possibility to be respected as they were feared. My father used to say the only cure for happenstance was preparation, and I had taken that lesson to heart.

Briar was conspicuously absent the while, and I knew there was a reason. But there was nothing left to do.

The nights got colder.

The rain came in.

And soon, it was time to go.

Seventeen

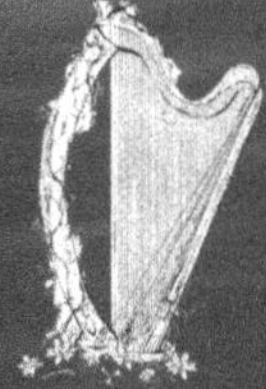

Emain Macha hadn't changed a whit in the near-two decades I'd been gone. My father's colors still hung from the high timber walls of the central keep, a flaming red hand on a white field— the Red Fist of Ulaid. We passed beneath the high city gates at the northern end along with the other wagons we'd met up with on the high road. It seemed the entire north had gathered to wish the new king and his bride happiness. Well, that and turn a few coins in the meantime.

Breccan had been right.

There were so many merchants, I'd never seen Emain Macha so full of color and life. Not even my father's marriage to Ælla's niece had produced so many vivid tents, stalls, criers, and hawkers. I supposed my cousin Niall was rather well-loved in Ulaid, though I hadn't heard much about him. His bride was rumored to be a great beauty but that was the extent of what I'd heard. Even though my blood pulsed with fear and horrible memories, I rather hoped I'd get a glimpse of the young couple before the celebration was over.

For no other reason than it might be nice to see some of my family members happy.

Breccan had helped me load my wagon, as promised, and we traveled with the bulk of our town's merchants and farmers. Wagon trains wound their way into the city from every direction, some bearing silks from the trading ports in the south, some sealskins and abalone from the west. Our humble procession bore mainly sheep, wool, and textiles from the colder northern reaches. We shuffled beneath the main portcullis I remembered so well from my youth, and were immediately ushered into the main mercantile square at the city's center; a large open-air courtyard with several premade stalls facing each other around the city's main water source.

As it had been in my youth, the town square was divided into regions: east, west, north, and south with Emain Macha's own mercantiles and furriers occupying the central courtyard— the most desirable spot. There was such a throng of merchants, many of our stalls had to be hastily raised along the one of the four connecting lanes racing through the city in each principal direction. Most of those who lived within the keep wouldn't make it down to the main square to browse our stalls, which would suit me just fine. The finest hawkers, those bearing precious metals, swords, and other finery would set up camp directly within the keep's main courtyard.

Although the fear lessened considerably the longer we were in town, deep down, I knew it might only take one person to remember King Muirdagh and his wild, fey daughter for me to end up right where I'd started. I'd worried my nails bloody by the time the chamberlain escorted our group to our stalls at the north end of the square.

Breccan performed double duty, helping both me and his father set up for the event. His stepmother had opted to stay home with her youngest children, which made Breccan quite happy. His father and I didn't speak much, but he had the stall next to mine, and caught me staring worriedly up at the keep. "They don't come down here much," he assured me with a kindly grin.

I'd always liked Breccan's father, even if he had questionable taste in women.

I mean, who was I to judge another's tastes?

I pulled my fingers out of my mouth. "Who doesn't?"

"Them royals. We might catch some of their maids and servants, though." He winked. "Won't that be nice?"

"Aye." I meant it, too. If the High King's daughter bought some of my scarves and shawls, I might open a shop back home and teach others to earn my coin for me when my eyesight got too bad. "It would."

Of course, I kept my long black hair braided up tight, and a woolen cap pulled low over my brow and ears. Just in case.

After a day of setting up and moving around without incident, the knot in my guts loosened, coil by coil. We spent the night in tents camped outside the city walls, tucked in close for warmth and safety. Those who could afford to, like Breccan's father, rented rooms at

The Singing Salmon down the docks, or other establishments that catered to the mercantile set. Since I'd spent nearly every coin I had to come here, I was not one of these. I didn't mind camping outside. It made me much less nervous about being there, and besides, the women from our town stuck together in tight groups. None left to use the privy tents nor wandered far on their own.

My own humble accommodations were nestled between Siobhán, the candlestick maker, and Dalla, the cobbler's wife. Neither were overly talkative, like me, but we had an unspoken understanding to look out for one another. After a quick visit to the privy tent together, the three of us headed to a quiet tavern at the foot of the hill, where Breccan was playing that night. The sign outside was too worn to read but that hardly stopped people from visiting by the cartload. The low-ceilinged taproom was filled with patrons, from narrow wall to narrow wall. Cheap ale and whiting stew seemed to be the main fare, but the rushes were clean, and the food was worth the two coppers I'd paid for a bowl. Auditions would begin at the keep bright and early the next day, and Breccan was grateful for the practice.

He tuned his harp, blushing adorably until he spied us in the crowd. We cheered him, as proud of him as we'd be of any of our own children. His father observed from a stool nearby, only partway frowning, which was progress, you ask me.

Maybe the boy could move back home soon, before every one of the baker's daughters wound up in the family way.

Breccan strummed his first chord, and the onlookers sighed. He *was* very talented, his fingers flying over the strings like hummingbird wings.

He sang:

> *Her eyes were a warning*
>
> *A young man ought to see*
>
> *Her lips bright as an apple*
>
> *Her hips wide as the sea*

Breccan's beautiful, rich voice carried over the crowd, crooning and forlorn. Several women nearby hummed appreciably.

> *But her red lips dripped with poison*
>
> *Her heart, cold as the sea*
>
> *And in my hour of dying*
>
> *I shan't forget what she said to me*

Breccan picked up the tempo, thumping his heel into the floorboards for a jaunty backbeat.

> *Oh, take thee off I beg thee*
>
> *Ye foul and worthless cheat*
>
> *My sisters have thee bedded*
>
> *My coin did thee keep*
>
> *Away, away*
>
> *Be gone*
>
> *To The Others I send thee*

The crowd howled with delight. While no Eirean would ever turn their nose up at a ballad, bawdy tunes were best loved. Everyone started clapping and stamping their feet while Breccan leaned into his playing. My companions, Siobhán and Dalla, chuckled into their tankards. Siobhán was also a widow like me (supposedly), and she was still handsome enough. Men sat too close, trying very hard to engage her in conversation until one, a pleasant looking fellow managed to hold her attention. Dalla raised bushy gray brows at me over her tankard, and I smirked back.

I'd lost a bet.

But there was time yet.

I might win my coin back.

Siobhán might still pour the man's ale over his cap and take her leave. Someone bumped my elbow then, spilling ale on my sleeve.

Away, away

Be gone

To The Others I send thee

Breccan sang on, gesticulating in mock desperation.

I cursed, and a man leaned over with a kerchief.

"My apologies, madam," he said, his voice summoning a marrow-deep shiver.

I cut my eyes at him.

"What are you *doing* here?" I hissed, hoping Dalla didn't look over. Briar took the seat next to me, dressed humbly in a worn brown tunic and brown suede leggings that had seen too many seasons. He wore a cap over his silver hair, which he'd either tucked under the brim or had magicked away for the evening. His eyes had lost their changeable luster. He even wore stubble on his chin, and fine crow's feet around his eyes. He was the same yet different enough, he might have been a harmless mortal man rather than the bane of my life. The bastard had the gall to smirk sideways at me. His disguise was good, very good, but not good enough.

Dalla noted him with some interest, as did every other woman within a mile of my table.

I sank into my seat like it might help me vanish.

"Get out of here!"

"No." He smiled, sipping his ale. "I love to hear the lad play."

I scoffed but couldn't argue.

Anyone with ears couldn't help but be enchanted by Breccan's playing. He was simply wonderful. Just as his tune reached a fine fever pitch, he stopped, spun around and with a painfully disappointed expression, resumed his mournful love ballad.

> *My love, how she wounds me*
>
> *Her bright eyes but a lie*
>
> *Her brothers soon to find me*
>
> *My blood they vow to shed*
>
> *Oh! But how shall I live without thee?*
>
> *Where shall I lay mine head*
>
> *In what bower do I slumber*
>
> *If she be not with me*

"None but Aenghus Óg should have hands so skilled," Briar noted, with a hard squint. Then, Breccan spun about again, stomping his feet. The crowd joined in, clapping and singing along.

Away, away

Be gone

To The Others I send thee

Away, away

Be gone

To The Others I send thee

Breccan finished his song and took an exaggerated bow, beaming. The crowd roared. "Thank you," he said, blushing furiously. "Shall I play something more?"

Briar cupped a hand over his mouth. "A ballad, *Midhir and Étaíne*."

I groaned, covering my face with my hands.

Breccan swept his harp high, his hands whispering mournfully over the strings.

"Can you begone, please?" I asked Briar, aside.

"No," he repeated, tipping his tankard into mine. "I'm protecting you."

"From what? Tomorrow's headache?"

He glanced around with narrowed eyes. "Wolves?"

I sucked my teeth at him. "There's greater risk of that at home, obviously."

"Not the four-legged kind."

I laughed out loud, and Dalla could stand it no longer. She leaned in. "Ciara, who's your friend, then?"

Briar took her hand as any peer might do. I watched the older woman go red to the roots of her hair.

"Just a fellow traveler, madam. Coffey's my name."

"Dalla," she returned, looking from him to me and back again. "You meet in the caravan?"

"Oh, yes," he lied. "Though we've met a time or two in other markets, haven't we, *Ciara*?"

I bobbed my head not trusting myself to be convincing.

"Well, isn't that nice?" said Dalla, subtly scooting her chair closer to Siobhán's with an encouraging smile.

Beneath our table, I kicked Briar's shoe.

"Now she thinks we're courting, you idiot."

He didn't say anything for a while, just gave me that long stare that made me uncomfortable. "Would that be so bad?"

I glared at him. "Just because I spoke to you once in fifteen years does *not* mean you get to invite yourself into my company whenever you feel like it."

"You don't want to be alone here any more than I want you here at all. You may lie to yourself, but never to me."

I wished no one was around so I could slap the know-it-all leer from his face.

"Why are you here, really?"

He took a long pull from his tankard and set it down. "I can't see the future, you know."

"Can't you?"

He shrugged. "Bits and pieces occur to me now and then, but usually, no."

"Are you telling me I need to worry?"

He shook his head. "No, I'm telling you *I* am worried." His tone gave me pause.

I sat for a long time, quietly squirming under his unwavering gaze. "What do you mean?"

But Breccan took a deep breath to sing the first verse of a mournful yarn, his voice so lovely and sad it cast a haze over the crowd. All the while, Briar stared a hole through my resolve.

I fidgeted over my tankard.

"What?" I asked, unsure where to look.

"Beware the strands," he said, as if quoting from a spell.

I had no idea how to answer that, and when I turned to tell him to make his prophecies more clear, he was gone. I looked around but knew I'd never find him. Breccan's song finished and we northerners stood, cheering. My cousin Niall was a fool if he did not choose the lad for his wedding feast. Even Breccan's father clapped, sniffling into his shirtsleeves.

On the way back to our tent village, I couldn't help but brood over Briar's warning.

Beware the strands?

I didn't have the first idea what in the hells that was supposed to mean. And it kept me up all night, mulling it over.

That, and the subtle ache blooming in my ice-cold chest.

IN THE MORNING, BRECCAN TOOK HIS LEAVE TO AUDITION with the rest of Ulaid's bards and players. We cheered him on his way uphill to the keep like a conquering hero, then set about our first market day with scarcely a breath between the two events. People from all over Eire had come to Emain Macha for the King of Ulaid's wedding. The taverns and inns were full up, and tents started popping up all around the lough. Many strange accents could be identified both in and outside the city walls, and we'd heard even merchants from Bretagne had sailed to Eire for the occasion. The High King himself had made the trip, I was told, as had King Mark's son, Lleu, and some of the native Norse lords from the south. I had no fear that Hester would be among them, as she was long dead, and her uncle Ælla had been slain in Northumberland years ago.

As the day wore on, we were all so busy I forgot to be afraid. I had prepared over five-hundred items for the trip, and burned through nearly a quarter of these by the end of the first day — and we had arrived early. Most of the wedding guests, including the bride, had yet to appear in Emain Macha. Their caravan was like-ly to show up in the morning the next day, and by then we merchants would have one additional preparation day before the crowds descended upon us like flies.

At the close of the third day, the King of Ulaid would be wed, the feasting would go on into the wee hours of the night, and we'd be expected to be packed up and on the road north again by noon on the fourth day. I rubbed the aching small of my back after just the first day and hoped I was ready for the rush. I thought about hiring one of Dalla's girls to help greet customers, since she had brought all four along. Just when I wondered how Breccan's audition had fared, I caught sight of his red head racing toward me through the parting crowd. His face said all before he spoken a word, and I grinned.

"You did it then?"

"I did!" He dimpled, clutching his side. He must have run all the way from the great hall. I clenched my abdomen rather than allow any memories to slink into my mind's eye.

"I knew you would," I said, throwing my arms around him. He'd gotten so tall it wasn't as easy as it had once been. "Tell me everything."

"Well, when we were first shown inside the keep, I could scarcely still my nerves. There were over a dozen players, all told, and many of them were quite talented."

I handed him half of my tart to prod him on.

"Anyway," he smacked around his bite, "I stood there, sticking out like a red thumb, looking around. What a hall! Such long timbers. I dunno where they prised such grand lumber from but it surely wasn't from the trees 'round Ulaid."

They came from Cymru and as far away as Bretagne, actually. Ulaid had trees aplenty, but mostly of the rowan, birch, and pine varieties. For good, solid hardwoods, we traded with other nations. My father had been most proud of the grandiosity of his hall. But I held my tongue. To one such as Breccan who'd grown up well outside of the capital, Uí Néill's keep would have seemed grand, indeed.

"The King is a rather imposing fellow. I nearly missed my name being called for how long I stared up at him, trying to glean why they call him the 'Black Knee.' They say he'll be high king one day, you know, after marrying old Áed's daughter. Many in the hall whisper he's a finer fit for the throne than Áed's son Murchad. Anyway, all the bards before me played and sang such beautiful, sad ballads, I admit to being intimidated. When I finally made it to the front, the King looked properly bleary-eyed. I felt certain he would reject us all for sheer boredom. But," he laughed, winking, "I had an inkling something jaunty might pick his face up from the floor."

"And it did, no doubt?"

"Of course, it did!" He beamed, gesticulating wildly. "So, I set my harp down at my feet and pulled out my tin whistle. Set in one or two sallies from *The Sailor's Wife*, then *Misty Eyed Maid*— had his foot tapping in a trice! I didn't even have to pick up my harp once before he clapped me into the gallery."

I squealed and mussed his hair. "I'm so proud of you!"

He spun me around until I was dizzy then set me down, brown eyes gleaming. "I'll get seven silvers for the day's work and can invite guests to watch the show from the gallery wing."

I was so happy for him, I barely noticed that there'd been a question in there.

"Well, what do you think?" He prodded, his cheeks red with mirth.

"About?"

He rolled his eyes. "You'll come and watch me play, won't you? I've asked my father already, and am hoping Siobhán will come too. Dalla said she and the girls have too many goods to load that night.

He must have seen my face fall.

"Ciara, what's wrong?"

He wanted me in the hall. My father's hall, where my previous life had ended in such a brutal, horrible way.

"I don't— know…" I muttered, noncommittally.

"Oh, but you must come!" he whined. "I will be far too nervous to play without everyone there. Please, Ciara. Siobhán may still refuse, and my father hasn't agreed to come, either."

I bit my lip so hard, I was sure to leave a mark. And I almost told him then, eyes darting around in fear, why I couldn't come. But he stared at me with such hopeful need, I kept my tongue behind my teeth. This was Breccan's first real chance to follow his dreams.

Had I not encouraged him every step of the way?

Helped him to purchase the harp on his back.

Taught what courtly songs I knew?

I had no business refusing him now. Besides, if his father didn't show, I'd likely be the only one he knew in there to support him. The anxiety burned in my gut for a long moment before I finally nodded.

"How could I refuse?"

Eighteen

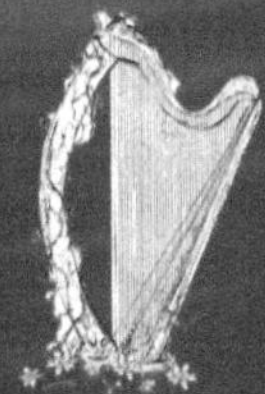

That night, I sat up in my tent. My nails were sore and bleeding, I'd worried them so. I paced for an hour or more, but that only made me need to relieve myself and even the walk to the baths and back did nothing to still my nerves. In my mind's eye, Máel's head tilted forward, then fell. At some point, I gave up and dutifully sorted my linens and shawls. Even that wasn't tedious enough a task to make me tired, and I was back to pacing before long. After a lifetime of counting the dust motes above my head, I lay in my bed feeling an overwhelming urge to scream, swiftly followed by the need to weep.

What was I going to do?

Though it seemed unlikely anyone in the room would recognize me now, I would still know exactly who I was. I would see my father seated in the center of the dais, smirking into his ale, his black mustache glinting red in the firelight. I would see Hester sitting beside him, prim, disinterested, and coolly handsome. I would see the men laughing and singing songs at supper, faces greasy with smeared grouse and lamb, eyes merry. I would hear their songs, their fists banging into their benches, cheering the Uí Néill.

I would see Calanthe's golden head bobbing to music, her white teeth flashing in a dimpled grin.

I would see her milky eye, reflecting the clouds above.

I did weep then, for a while.

For my sister who didn't deserve the cruel fate I had wished upon her.

For my father, whose life ended sadly, in disgrace.

For my stepmother who had been right to accuse me.

For Cook, who'd died in anonymity to protect me.

For myself, for being such a foolish, self-interested child.

"Deirdre," whispered Briar from the dark.

I wasn't surprised to hear he was there. He always seemed to be near whenever I was about to do something I'd regret forever. A warm hand reached from the shadows, sliding over mine.

"You are not alone."

He'd said that before.

But of course I *was*. I had never been so alone in my life, not even when Cook passed and left me to face the long winters on my own. There was no one left. They had all gone, because of me… because of my sin.

"Please don't go," Briar pleaded. "I see how it pains you."

"I gave my word."

"Breccan will understand, if you tell him the truth."

I pushed myself up on my elbow. "Are you mad?"

"Your truth, then. Tell him you cannot face your ghosts."

"I can't." I sniffed.

"You are not his mother."

"I know that!" I snapped. "But I love him, all the same."

"Yes," Briar admitted, sadly. He fell silent after, his hand on mine. I lay back down, turning my face into the tent wall.

"Will you tell me what you meant?"

"About what?"

"'The strands.'"

I felt him shift uncomfortably beside me.

"That is all I know."

"Don't lie."

"I have never lied to you, Deirdre, and never shall."

"But you have a bad feeling?"

"Yes," he said, his voice soft.

"I can't leave," I told him.

"I know."

I was silent for a long time, imagining all the ways in which I would keep well out of sight, where I would stand to not be seen, how quiet I would be. I could linger for just one song, make sure Breccan saw me, and then slip out of the keep through the kitchen and back to my tent to pack— quick as a breeze.

I could do this.

I would do it.

It was well past the darkest part of the night when I felt Briar stand. Without thinking, I reached out and caught his sleeve.

"Stay with me, for just a while more?"

Wordless, he returned to my side, tucking his warm length against my back. After a while, my shivering stopped, and I fell into a blessedly dreamless sleep.

THE KEEP WAS SMALLER THAN I RECALLED, AS IF IT HAD somehow deflated in my absence, like a shrunken gourd. With my heart in my throat, I followed the crowd of well-wishers and guests on their long climb up the slope to the keep. Its black-weather-stained timbers perched at the top of Macha's second twin, ominous as a bird of prey. At its pinnacle, waved the red fist of Ulaid. As I was swept beneath the heavy iron gate, I took several deep breaths.

You can do this.

No one even knows you exist.

The crush inside the inner bailey kept me squeezed against the high timber walls, unable to pause or gawp. There were so many people I feared to trip lest I be trampled. It seemed everyone with a marginally decent shirt and pair of shoes was busy trying to gain entry into the hall at the gate. There had to be at least three-hundred people clamoring for entry, with and without passes. Those without were summarily shoved aside and ordered to vacate the keep. Anyone who resisted was tossed out by the king's warriors.

Looking down at my empty hands, I realized I too lacked a pass. I spent a few moments twiddling my scabbed thumbs before I decided on another course of action. Rather than wait around to be denied entry or answer any number of uncomfortable questions, I knew another way in. One that would draw very little attention.

I slipped around the rear right corner to the kitchens.

As I suspected, the way was mostly clear, save for a few guards gathered along the wall, laughing and generally not paying attention. A few kitchen girls raced back and forth with pots, baskets, laundry, and other feast-day chores. Without a moment's hesitation, I stooped to pick up a basket of freshly folded-linens and carried them inside to the overheated kitchens. There were so many maids and servers dashing about, no one had a spare moment to be concerned about me. I was already well inside the stone walls of the main residence before I gave myself permission to breathe.

Knowing exactly where the laundry was, I kept going, dodging maids, warriors, and any other human furniture in my way. Around the north corner, past the armory, I descended a set of low stone stairs. It looked very much the same as it always had. So much so, that I felt a deep pang for the well-worn flagstones at my feet, the dusty timbers that held up the ceiling. It even smelled the same, a combination of damp, lamp oil and tallow, onions and burdock from the kitchens. The cavernous chamber was stuffed to the brim with women, grooms, and linens stacked around large wooden vats lined with hammered bronze, and filled with boiling piss and soap flakes. The taners down in the town below the keep turned record profts bartering human urine with the king's stewards when I lived here. Nothing could lift blood, muck, or sweat from a tunic quite so neatly... if only it didn't smell so terrible.

My nose twitched something awful.

Quick as a hare, I set my basket down and backed out nearly as fast as I'd come in. I was sneezing when I came up a second set of stairs leading directly to the hall. If I thought the courtyard was packed, I hadn't seen anything yet. In all my years here, I had never observed the hall so full of guests. Every table, chair, nook, and cranny had been claimed. There was scarcely space to breathe without someone's elbow jabbing into one's ribs.

And the heat! Gods, I had forgotten how overheated the hall could be during feast days. Sweat was already trickling down my spine by the time I made it through the great oak doorway. As carefully as I could, I crept around the incredible press of people to get to the gallery staircase. This too, was packed with revelers, some common, some noble— all seemingly inebriated or in very good spirits. Rather than be flattened in the doorway, I politely pushed my way through to the wooden gallery stairs on my right. The musician's box had an elevated seat just above the dais, and it was here that I found Breccan and Siobhán, down at the far end. Relieved, I made my way over to them swallowing my heart back into my chest. Breccan beamed when he saw me. Siobhán was busy fixing a tear in the fine tunic I'd made him, her blond brows drawn together in concentration.

I did not look down.

"Ciara!" he exclaimed, and made as if to grab me in a bear hug. Siobhán hissed at him past the thread in her teeth, forcing him to be still. "I was worried you wouldn't make it. There was such a crush at the gate, someone struck me in the eye, and one of my strings snapped." He nodded to his harp, leaning against the window box.

The other musicians in the gallery were busy preparing their own costumes and instruments, eying Breccan's spot with envy. Nearly half a dozen men stood nearly elbow to elbow in the narrow, cramped, poorly lit space.

"Thankfully," Siobhán said, glaring back at each of them. "We got here early, else we might have no room to breathe let alone restring a harp."

Those strings had cost him nearly a year's wages at the bakery, I recalled.

"What are you going to do?" I asked, suddenly worried.

His eyes twinkled. "I have a backup plan."

My brows raised. That sounded ominous.

"Breccan, you didn't?" I looked around, hoping not to spot a miffed musician missing a set of strings. Breccan wasn't a thief, per say, but he did have funny ideas about 'borrowing' that had gotten him into trouble more times than I could count.

He waved me away. "Nothing so bad as that."

But I didn't like the way his mouth crooked up at the corner. Siobhán and I shared an exasperated glance over his shoulder. I opened my mouth to give him the warning he definitely needed to hear, but before I could utter a word, a cry went up in the gallery below. The king and his new queen swept into the hall. The cheers were deafening.

Try as I might to avoid the temptation to peek down into my past and missed future, I couldn't help but look.

My cousin Niall was dark-haired, like my father, but had a hawkish nose and startlingly bright eyes. He was very tall, indeed, and had a wicked scar running the length of his cheek. He was a famed warrior, after all, as no Uí Néill king could hope to ascend without having proved themselves as a warrior. He carried a longsword at his hip in the norse fashion belted over a silver shortaxe. A luxurious black bearskin draped over his shoulders, clasped together by a heavy golden torc.

And upon his brow, my father's beaten iron fillet.

He grinned as he came into the room, appearing genuinely pleased. He was handsome, but not so handsome as my father had been. Beside him was the loveliest woman I'd ever seen, aside from Calanthe. The High King's daughter Roana shone bright as sunrise over the lough. Rich, wild curls framed her curves like a burning red cloak. Eyes like dark gems flashed from a smiling, oval-shaped face. She wore white, in deference to Uí Néill tradition, which her new subjects were sure to appreciate. The din was deafening as the startling new couple moved proudly to the dais, arm in arm. I had heard it said that my cousin fought quite hard to win his bride. No one in the hall could be at a loss to wonder why. They cut fine, elegant figures as they took their seats, hands clasped. My father's seat. She sat in the very same chair I had during every feast in this room, save my last. A rushing surge of memories threatened to choke me. I clenched my fists and willed my mind to silence.

The king raised his cup and the crowd quieted.

"Ulaid, I give you my Queen!"

One of my eardrums threatened to pop. The crowd took several minutes to calm down again. Breccan leaned over the railing, grinning. Siobhán dabbed at her eyes. After what felt like an eternity, he slammed his cup down with a wide grin.

"Let's eat and have some music, hey?"

The crowd roared. I plugged my ears that time, lest I lose all hearing.

Breccan shifted to me, nerves apparent on his face.

"I must restring. Can you—"

I looked around at the other musicians all jockeying for position and room to prepare. There were lutists, flute players, bodhran players, and one or two singers. Some of them came in a group to play background music for the king's feast. These set up at the railing and were already playing a light, but merry tune. Others, only four or so, came to perform solo, as Breccan had done. However, Breccan was the only one I could see that played more than one instrument on his own. I couldn't stave off the pride that swelled in my chest.

He was not my son, but he was certainly the closest I'd ever get to one.

"Yes, Siobhán and I will watch for the harper's call. But you be quick about it. Best not to start a brawl at your debut."

One lutist was already sizing us up for weakness. His eyes narrow, calculating. We had the best spot in the gallery, and he was squeezed uncomfortably between two flutists who kept jabbing him with their elbows.

Siobhán wagged a finger at him. "I'd think again, if I were you, friend," she warned. She was shorter than me, so I edged around her. We presented a stern barrier to Breccan's competition. For that matter, I couldn't see what Breccan was doing over my shoulder, only that he was crouched down in the far corner, winding something golden around his broken string. I hoped whatever it was would hold and not shame him before the king. All during the feast, Siobhán and I stood guard while Breccan prepared for the most important night of his life.

I was so concerned about his fate, I'd forgotten to be wary of my own.

Nineteen

When the feasting was done, the king called for entertainment. The jesters and mummers, as always, came first. They tumbled through the crowd to the center of the hall beneath the dais, japing and jongling. The new queen laughed, a delightful, cheerful sound. The king smiled in such a way that I immediately understood he was more pleased by her happiness than he cared for the festivities. It elevated my opinion of him, to say the least. My father had always been good to Hester, but theirs had been a very reserved marriage. He had been happy with her for years, as I'd often lamented in my youth. But I think he came to love her less as the years waned on.

Looking down at this new queen, I hoped for her sake, their joy was long lived.

Ulaid could do with a happy tale after so much sorrow.

The mummers came after the jongleurs, bowing to each corner of the hall. Faces painted in garish colors with exaggerated expressions etched over their brows, four of them swept off their heavy robes to display vibrant costumes. One wore a deep blue cloak with an iron fillet upon his crown, the other a Dane's leather cuirass and fur boots.

Ah, I thought. *They are telling my father's story.*

Here was great Matudán, meeting Ælla at the muddy An Ruirthech river. They crossed swords and Ælla, beaten, fled south of the river. The mummers depicted this momentous event by waving a woolen blue blanket beside two wooden horses mounted on sticks. They fled behind a makeshift curtain, and came out again, this time with mighty Muirdagh beating Ælla back to the sea. Then, from behind the curtain, came the garish and slightly comical version of my stepmother. Hester demurely entered the stage, exaggeratedly distracting my father. From the other side of the curtain came a dark-haired woman, comically pleading with my father not to look. This would be my mother.

My cheeks reddened and my gut hardened like lead.

My 'mother' clutched at my father's cloak, but he would not look away from the golden-haired Danish princess. Ælla, dramatically stroking his beard, presented Hester to my father but warned him he could not keep his Eirean consort. My father coolly set my mother aside clinging to his new prize. They retreated behind the curtain, leaving my mother's avatar alone, weeping on the stage. The crowd jeered at her, for they knew what came next. The mummers pulled a dark blanket behind her while another held a silver serving dish up to represent the moon. My mother drew a shiny dagger, holding it aloft before swiftly plunging it into her breast. From behind her, a dark figure caught her as she fell, visibly vowing to exact her vengeance as she died.

The crowd hissed and booed.

This wasn't how my mother died at all, in fact, she'd died before my father ever challenged Ælla at the border or met Hester in her uncle's camp— but I supposed the people had to find a means to explain what would happen later. How I became the curse that brought my father's house low. Fascinated as I was repulsed, I couldn't look away.

The mummers changed the scene.

The king and queen clapped.

Now, what was meant to be a young, fair-haired girl took the stage. She picked wildflowers beneath a golden serving dish meant to represent the sun. The queen giggled at something the king whispered to her. His warriors thrummed their tables with their knuckles. Everyone had always loved Calanthe. They loved her still. The fact didn't pain me as it used to. She had been a lovable, bright girl with an easy smile and a warm heart. I missed her too. I bit my tongue to keep the tears from my eyes.

The blue blanket was out again, this time spread wide to represent the lough. Calanthe hummed while plucking scattered linen blooms beneath her feet, when a warrior strode onto the stage, all masculine swagger and mustachioed elegance I bit back a sob. Siobhán glanced over at me. I dug what was left of my nails into my palms hard enough to cut the feeling from my fingers. 'Máel' swept Calanthe a grand bow. The two then danced together in the meadow for a time, until he pleaded her his troth. From behind the curtain, a dark-haired girl with a sour expression crept onto the stage, spying on the young lovers.

This version of me tore at her hair and gnawed at her hands.

Well, at least it was partially accurate.

This 'me' was clearly jealous and spiteful of my beautiful sister. When Máel turned away from the scene, the figure grasped Calanthe's shoulders and tossed her into the blanket posing as the lough. The crowd booed and stamped their feet. The wicked me retreated behind the curtain but emerged again from the other side, just as Máel and my father met on the shore. Máel made his pleading gestures, but my actor leaned in to whisper in my father's ear.

My father violently waved Máel's request away. 'Deirdre' dramatically stepped forward instead, the eldest daughter, to take the space beside him. Backlit from behind the curtain by a flickering oil lamp, the dark, sinister shape came once again, to clasp the couple's hands together. Just then, Calanthe's body was dragged onto the stage. The actor was wet all over. The straw they used to mimic her golden hair dripped all over the dais to make thick puddles at the base of the steps. The actor portraying Hester gestured her extreme grief— mad-eyed and vicious.

And the rest of the tale, you already know.

It took all of my strength not to weep, wail, or shout down how wrong the mummers had got my story. When the actor portraying my father swept his wooden sword across Máel's throat, I felt sick. I slid down the railing to take a seat on the dusty wooden floorboards, my back to the mummery below. Breccan knelt in front of me, suddenly very concerned. Siobhán was already there. She gave me a look that told me she was far sharper than she let on.

Women always were.

"Ciara, are you all right?" Breccan asked.

I nodded. "I'm fine. Just the heat of the braziers, is all."

"Oh, right. It is overwarm and close in here. Do you need to go outside? I think the king won't call the bards down for some time, so I could—"

"No," Siobhán answered for me, winding her hand through mine. "She'll be fine in a moment. You should get ready, Breccan."

He flushed. "Ah, right. You sure?"

"Yes," I croaked. "I'll be watching. Don't you dare shame me."

He grinned. "Right you are."

After he'd stood and moved away, Siobhán wrapped an arm around me. She looked over her shoulder and then back to me.

"It's almost over."

I nodded.

"For the record, I know it didn't happen this way."

I looked up. "How do you know?"

"Most of us do. We're not all fools… Ciara."

I struggled a bit with my reply.

What could I say?

"It is a sad tale."

"Indeed."

She waited a moment for me to collect myself.

"Should we take a turn outside?"

I wiped my nose and stood up, back still to the dreaded scene below. I had brought this upon myself, after all. No point behaving like a child now. "No, it was hard enough to get inside once. Best we stay."

Siobhán patted my shoulder.

"Right."But her eyes swam with knowledge, indignation, and perhaps pity. "You aren't the only... *Southerner*... in our village."

Her meaning was plain.

She'd been banished to the North as I had been.

We stared at each other for quite a while, saying nothing.

So, she was like me.

Someone's unmarried daughter.

Someone's undutiful wife.

Someone's unwanted sister.

Someone's unruly leman.

Someone's unrepentant witch.

Noble, too, if I caught her meaning.

I wanted to ask her true name, but knew she couldn't share it. Not here. Not in the belly of the beast with so many kinsmen to hand. For surely, if she had surviving kin, they were here to serve my cousin as every noble must.

"The black bull." She sniffed, as if reading my thoughts, and jerking her chin at the far corner of the hall.

There, a handful of men and women sat, eying those nearer the dais with palatable envy.

"Right," I said.

Breifne, from the opposite coast.

Rather than answer, I dragged my eyes to the king's standard— the red fist.

"Thought so," she cooed back, gripping my elbow and turning me back to the scene below.

Thank Brida, the mummers had cleared, leaving only the bards and their endless, inane ballads to endure. Then I could leave and never set eyes on this place again. Her people were Ó Dónaills. My family's sworn rivals, although that old enmity seemed to have waned. She turned back to sneer down at them. None noticed.

"Disappointing lot, no?"

I made sure Breccan couldn't hear us before I answered. He was far away, tinkering with his strings. Whatever he used must have been pleasing, for he was smiling and whistling to himself.

"How long have you known?"

"About you? Oh, ages. Dalla knows, too. She was one of your mother's washerwomen."

I flushed to the roots of my hair.

"That long then?"

She shrugged. "We've met before. At your father's wedding. You wouldn't remember me as I was young and spirited then. Fancied myself in love with the wrong man. You see how that turned out." She swept a hand over her face, then patted my hand. "We'll get good and drunk when this is over and share our tales of woe."

We women.

We replaceable, unloved, unprecious objects.

What bad luck it was to be born female.

I squeezed her fingers just as the king banged his cup against the table, calling for his bards. I felt Breccan leap to action behind us. But just for that moment, Siobhán and I shared a lifetime of pain in a glance.

"I would be honored."

Siobhán smiled and leaned over the railing.

"We'll have to wait to watch our boy become the greatest bard in the land, first."

"Yes," I said, wiping the corner of my eyes.

Her family never once raised their heads in her direction.

Nor did any of mine.

If Niall had ever seen me, he'd long forgotten my face.

For the first time since we came to Emain Macha, I wasn't afraid. For that briefest span, I was no longer alone.

Of course, it could not last.

WE SAT THROUGH THREE MODERATELY TALENTED BARDS before it was Breccan's turn. As the youngest and least experienced among them, it was natural that he should be stone last. We didn't mind too much since we were enjoying ourselves. One of the lutists had brought a flagon of Bretagn red to mark the occasion, and shared it with everyone gathered in the gallery. My cheeks warmed and my heart had stopped threatening to burst from my chest.

I forgot which room I was in.

I stopped thinking about the mummer's farce.

I ceased to worry over being recognized.

Siobhán's shoulder next to mine, a cup of wine in my hand, a smile on my face; I simply forgot where I was and how afraid I should have been. The last bard told the most absurd, ribald stories we'd yet heard that night, and we laughed and clapped along with everyone else in the hall. Some of the gathered guests had cleared a few benches and tables and led their wives, daughters, and sweethearts onto the flagstones. The king and his new bride, included. A gentleman leaned in to ask Siobhán down, but she waved him off, accepting a third cup of wine instead. It occurred to me then, that this was what camaraderie felt like.

I was unfamiliar.

But maybe I didn't have to be anymore? Siobhán watched me sidelong for a while, as if she understood what I was thinking.

"Not so bad then?"

I shook my head, and she laughed.

We were still standing there smiling like a pair of fools when Breccan made his way to the raised stage below the dais.

Despite their mutual gripe over his finding the best spot to prepare and rehearse, the musician's gallery all cheered the lad on.

Breccan beamed up at us, his eyes nervous but hopeful.

The king brightened as soon as he saw him.

"Ah!" he exclaimed. "This is the lad I told you about, my love." I heard him say to his queen.

Roana, likely soused far past her wits, and red-cheeked as an apple, raised her cup. "Play us something lively, young bard."

Breccan bowed, picked up his flute, and did as he was bid.

The whole hall came together, clapping and humming along.

The young queen, it seemed, loved to dance. She led the king through another jaunty jig, and I accepted my fourth cup of wine. The next tune was equally as vivacious and the one after that, even more so. By turns, the queen flung herself into her chair in a fit of giggles. The king kissed her hand and leaned over to speak to his chamberlain. Breccan, not knowing if he was dismissed, made to grab his things and exit the stage. But the queen called out, "Wait! We'd have more of you yet, young bard."

Her voice chimed like a string of bells.

At that moment, a sudden chill slithered into my heart. I stopped mid-sip and turned.

Breccan bowed from the waist, awkwardly, of course. "What would my queen care most to hear?"

"Your harp!" she cried, clasping her hands together. "Play us something lovely and sad."

"Yes," agreed the king. "A ballad, if you please, my wife commands it."

The hairs on my arms raised, though nothing appeared to be wrong. Seeing my discomfiture, Siobhán reached out to touch my arm; a question in her eyes.

Breccan reached for his harp.

The instrument wasn't a thing of beauty, but what it lacked in aesthetic charm it made up for in tone. At least, that's how things usually lay. Tonight, however, his harp was more than a hunk of faded wood with a heavily curved outpillar and horsehair strings.

Something radiant caught the light when he moved.

Something gleaming and golden.

Something that I should have noticed earlier.

Breccan's harp was strung with beautiful golden strings.

The lad didn't own a scrap of gold thread and never had, so far as I knew. They were so fine, in fact, they looked very much like hair. I felt all the warmth drain from my face. I dropped my cup and it clattered to the stone floor to bounce from a cousin of the High King's boot. He didn't notice. All eyes were on Breccan and his shining harp strings. They were a rich, luminous gold. A gold so radiant, it might absorb all the light in the hall.

Just as Calanthe had, so long ago.

I gripped the bannister so hard, it cracked beneath my nails. Breccan glanced up, sheepish and mischievous all at once. I wasn't smiling, but he didn't seem to care.

This was his moment.

Even if he'd stolen strands of my sister's hair to mark it.

Beware the strands, Briar whispered in my memory.

A familiar ice-cold dread caught in my throat.

In my head, I heard the bell again.

I drew in a sharp breath as if I might scream.

But it was already too late.

Breccan strummed his first note, and my world came undone.

For the second time.

THE HARP FILLED THE AIR WITH A SOMBER SOUND SO LOVELY, it wrenched a collective sigh from the gathering. The melody was unlike any we'd ever heard, an inhuman beauty both fallow and frail. Like a song tucked beneath a wave.

Or a deep, dark lough.

Breccan's hands flew over the strings like a man possessed, plucking notes not meant for mortal hands. Watching his face, I knew at once he was as alarmed as I. This wasn't his song.

His head whipped up, eyes large.

But his fingers didn't stop. Couldn't stop.

The song took on an impossibly maudlin pitch that forced tears from my eyes. Siobhán wept beside me, clutching her throat. The queen too, sobbed in her chair, covering her mouth. Another woman's heartwrenching wail filled the hall. The sound dragged every sadness

I'd ever experienced to the forefront of my mind, clawing into my heart and stopping the breath in my lungs. Siobhán sank to the floor, stifling a scream. The crowd cried out, skittering from their seats, falling all over themselves to get away.

The braziers abruptly went out. The torches snuffed. Only a soft greenish light broke the darkness in the hall, casting strange, underwater shadows over the walls and floor.

It came from Breccan's harp.

Alarmed, the king pulled his wife into the circle of his arms, dragging them both behind his chair. "Stop, boy! Stop playing!"

Face milk-white, Breccan's voice cracked. "I can't! Someone… someone *help me*!"

"It's The Others!" shouted one fellow.

"Kill the boy before he casts his spell!" moaned a second.

"He will curse us all!" bleated a woman nearby.

But no one dared move.

The song took on a terribly mournful timbre, and I too, felt my knees go to water.

Breccan begged, "It hurts, please! Please help me!"

An apparition materialized in the circle of pale, mottled light cast by Breccan's strings. A woman's face materialized above the harp's crown, her single eye shining white as a fish's belly. I think I moaned my sister's name then, but I can't recall.

For there she was, as battered as the day she died.

Breccan's nose bled and tears streamed down his face, but no one stopped him. The queen buried her face in her husband's arm. A serving girl fainted, wine pooling beneath her like blood. Another servant wept into her apron. Several of the men attempted to escape through the heavy oak doors at the end of the hall. But the doors slammed shut, sweeping most of them back to the floor. Everyone skittered or slid as far away from Breccan as they could.

My sister found her voice then.

A whisper as strong as a thunderclap yet soft as rain over a sandy shore:

Woe…

The voice sang.

Woe

Woe to the red hand

Woe to the king

> *Woe to his Queen*
>
> *And woe to my sister*
>
> *Deirdre*
>
> *Who murdered me*

The apparition flickered. I felt its eyes on me. Breccan's fingers bled over his strings.

> *Woe*
>
> *Woe to thee*
>
> *Woe to me*
>
> *And shame for all*
>
> *Who brave the Red Hand's Hall*

In utter horror, I stood transfixed, staring into Calanthe's remaining eye. I knew then, I would never be forgiven. I had no right to happiness, however small, for I had stolen hers. I shrank beneath that milky gaze, feeling the railing give way beneath my hands.

With a startled cry, Siobhán reached out and caught me by my belt before I could tumble to the flagstones below.

The eye watched only me.

I could not hide.

But just as violently as the apparition had appeared, the strings snapped beneath Breccan's bloodied fingers.

He collapsed, weeping over his ruined hand. Calanthe's image faded. The braziers burst aflame once more. The doors swung open. Like a herd of startled deer, people raced from the hall as if chased by hounds. Many cried out for the Gods as they crossed the threshold. Others ran to Breccan, weapons raised. He held up his ruined hand, his face wet with tears and snot. But they dragged him from the floor, crushing his harp beneath their boots.

"No!" he blubbered, unable to struggle. "I don't know what happened… I don't know!" As they manhandled him, his eyes darted around frantically until they locked on mine.

A small realization stretched his pupils wide.

"Ciara! Ciara! Tell them it wasn't me! Tell them!"

I clawed myself upright.

"Breccan! Don't hurt him! Stop!" I screeched, struggling to my feet.

Again, Siobhán caught me by the belt. "No, not here," she said into my nape. "They'll burn you both."

But I couldn't let them take Breccan!

He was only in this position because of my sin.

I had to do something!

I fought her, but Siobhán was sturdier than me. She tugged me after the fleeing musicians, toward the stairs. The king, having shoved his wife into the arms of one of her women, stretched himself to his full height. I saw him clearly when we made it to the base of the steps. His expression straddled the line between fear and outrage.

"You will burn for this, boy. How dare you bring your curses here, to my wife!" The king spat stomping behind his entourage, his hand on his sword hilt. He looked very like my father, just then. I didn't catch the rest of what he said before Siobhán half-pushed, half-dragged me through the terrified crowd. For several minutes, all I could see were the backs of expensive gowns, smell the sharp tang of sweat, and feel the pain of other people's heels connecting with my own ankles and toes in a desperate dash from the hall.

Many times, I stumbled, and Siobhán had to hook her arms under mine to lift me out of someone's path. I didn't realize I was weeping until I tasted salt. Somehow, we wound up exiting through the kitchen in the train of a few savvy nobles and waitstaff. And before I knew it, Siobhán was guiding me through the market toward the outer wall.

"We can't leave him."

"Shut your mouth till we're clear," she hissed over her shoulder.

"This is my fault. I need to go back."

She stopped short, jerking me behind a cart.

"Do you know what they'll do to you?"

"They'll do it to Breccan if I don't."

I'd never seen her face as pale as it was just then.

"They'll burn him no matter what you do. The queen's priests will see to it."

I had heard Roana followed the new religion, but had seen no evidence of such tonight. Maybe I could speak to her. I knew how to get inside the keep.

Siobhán squeezed my wrist, hard. "Ciara, this is not the way. We need help."

"Who will help us?"

She blinked back at me, her jaw trembling.

She didn't know.

Neither did I.

"We'll think of something," she said, finally, resuming our march toward the merchant encampment.

Twenty

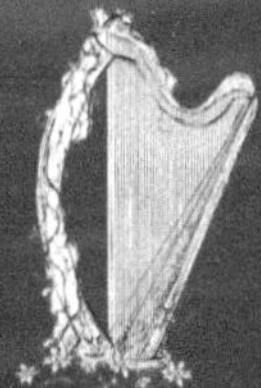

For the next two nights, Emain Macha collapsed in upon itself.

Villager turned on villager. Several suspected witches and fairies were arrested or dragged toward the dungeons without trial. Families put the elderly out of their homes. Sick children were led outside the gates and abandoned. Every house closed their shutters and set candles within carved turnips to frighten spirits from their doorstops. The streets filled with soldiers. Many townsfolk fled. Some remained, gathered outside the keep day and night, baying for Breccan's blood. The Others inspired such fear, everyone believed the city and its new king were cursed.

Much like the last king.

The fey-touched were doomed, all knew. The house of Uí Néill must make amends or be torn from their seat. As someone who'd lost everything to fairy magic, I couldn't say paranoia like this wasn't earned. While the rest of our village swiftly packed their things and fled home, only Breccan's father, Siobhán, and I stayed behind. Breccan's father tried to beg an audience with the king on multiple occasions but had been beaten from the gates each time. The last beating cost him the use of his right leg and the hearing in his left ear.

Siobhán and I pleaded with him to stop and let us think of another solution, but he blamed us for his son's fate. Hadn't I encouraged Breccan to take up music and verse, and taught him to sing? Hadn't Siobhán and the other townswomen coddled and cosseted the lad since he was a boy? Hadn't we all cheered him in his disobedience? Would Breccan be in this situation if we hadn't helped him get here?

His father had a point.

Wasn't he now suffering under a curse meant for me?

We tried everything we could. In town, I sold every scrap of linen I had, every shawl, and every ribbon and thread. Siobhán traded all she had left to spare, and sold her best boots and warmest cloak for whatever price she could fetch from twitchy merchants that would rather see our backs than our coin. When we had a tidy sum to barter with, we approached the town exchequer to beg or buy Breccan's release.

The fellow wouldn't even see us. His steward chased us down the street with an ash-hewn cane. Thinking we had the wrong man, we went to the mayor next, only to meet with the same treatment.

That morning, we'd gone to the captain of the city watch, pleading on our hands and knees. We offered him all the coin we had and more, if he would grant us an audience with the king. The captain had us thrashed at noon, five lashes each. Our shirts torn and bloodied from the back, we were forced to limp through the streets back to our tent. Two sad women, who drew more and more suspicion every moment they lingered in the city. We sat together all day, dazed and running shy of ideas. In the distance, we could hear the hammers pounding Breccan's pyre into place.

Every strike made me flinch.

They would burn him tomorrow at dawn.

Siobhán, her eyes sunken, stared at the tent wall from my cot. I sat on the dirt at her knee, idly toying with the useless coins in my purse. When I could bear it no longer, I kicked the bag over, spilling its contents over my foot. "I have no choice now, surely you see that?" I said, without turning around. "You should go home."

Siobhán laughed through her nose. "They'll kill you."

"I deserve it."

"Do you?" she asked, sneering down at me. "My brother was one of your father's vassals, you know. He was there that week, same as the rest of Ulaid's warriors. He knew Máel well enough to despise the fellow. He boasted of his conquest, you know? Told anyone who would listen that he had his pick of the king's get." She paused to snort. "Your sister was a stupid girl who killed herself over a man not fit to shovel her shite. You didn't do that to her."

It was my turn to sigh.

"What if I did meet one of The Others and he'd given me the power to ruin my whole family?"

Siobhán gave me a long, dry look. "You really believe that?"

"I know it."

She snorted again. "Maybe so. Wish I had that excuse."

"How so?"

"I was once like your sister. Vain, spoiled, and hungry to be seen. If I'd bothered to consider who might be watching, I might have thought better of my behavior."

"What happened to you?"

She shrugged. "What happens to every stupid girl who only dreams of being worshipped. A man happened. A man my father didn't approve of." She paused to twist her nose. "A priest, no less. If he'd been one of my father's men, he might have been coerced into wedding me when I grew round with his child. But not this one, no. He couldn't be forced to accept blame for our daughter. She died when she was born, but everyone already knew by then. So, he sent me off, and here we are."

"Whatever became of the priest?"

"I'm certain he and his piety are off somewhere seducing more stupid young girls, peppering the land with fatherless brats."

"I'm sorry."

"Don't be. As a 'widow,' I'm free to do what I want. Dance when I please, drink when I want to, and tup who I wish. That tonsured tomcat did me a favor."

"Would that I felt so."

"Why *don't* you?" Her head cocked at me, and eyebrow raised. "You're a wealthy woman, by northern standards. You've all your teeth, ten fingers and toes. You're even passing handsome, though perhaps not as striking as once you were. You live alone, make your own choices, sleep where you want to, and speak only when you feel like it. How is such a life any worse than marrying some rich oaf and squeezing out his brats until you die?"

"I suppose I hadn't thought of it like that." I smiled. "But you misunderstand me. I like my life as it is. I only wish others hadn't been made to suffer for my choices."

"We all suffer in our own way, Princess." She tugged a thumb behind her, toward the keep. "Breccan stole those strands from you. I know it, because I saw them in his satchel on the way down. He told me you wouldn't mind, and I should have asked you then. It didn't occur to me what a price he would pay for the theft."

I shifted uncomfortably in my seat, rubbing my torn fingers over my nose. "If I'd told him the truth, he wouldn't have been tempted."

"If you told him the truth, he would have laughed his fool head off and taken them anyway. You've known the lad for fifteen summers, but I helped his mother push him into the world. He's been a naughty boy since he drew his first breath, though we love him so. We never scolded him long or hard enough to correct him."

"He doesn't deserve what they will do to him."

"Aye, and neither do you."

I realized then that Siobhán was crying.

Slow, fat tears rolled down her sharp cheekbones.

Her eyes were full of regret.

She was leaving.

Her long fingers wound through mine. "Please, come with me. One mistake isn't worth two lives."

I was grateful to her.

She'd shared her story with me, without asking me to do the same. She let me keep my secrets close, and trusted me anyway. For a while, we sat together in silence. Our joined hands seemed to reach through time and circumstance; two fates bound by tragedy. "Will you take my pony back with you? She's a good girl who'll serve you well."

Siobhán heaved a heavy, resigned sigh, giving my fingers one last squeeze. "Yes, Deirdre Ap Muirdagh, I will."

SIOBHÁN TOOK HER LEAVE BEFORE SUNRISE.

She told me she wanted to stay longer, but hoped to make the next inn before nightfall. She'd lingered longer than she could afford to already, and would rather not remain to watch Breccan die. Again, she begged me to return with her, but my mind was set to my task. This was my fault. I would fix it if it killed me. I waved as she trotted down the road, mounted on Nell with most of my coin secretly tucked under her saddle. I wouldn't be needing it where I was headed. When I could no longer see her, I turned back to the keep.

Destiny beckoned.

Jaw set, I walked forward.

Before long, I felt someone beside me, matching my stride.

I didn't bother to look, for I knew very well who it was.

"*Beware the strands*, indeed."

"I didn't know, I swear it," Briar vowed, his tone pleading. "Deirdre, you can catch her. It's not too late."

I kept marching onward.

"I won't let him die for me."

Briar swore under his breath. "Will you not listen to reason? Calanthe's death was not your doing. A vengeful spirit has no concept of right or wrong, only what was felt as they passed. You don't owe her your death."

"No," I answered, surprised by the truth of my own admission. "But Breccan owes even less."

"Please, Deirdre. Don't do this," he begged, and I stopped to look at him. He wore his disguise but that was flimsy enough.

As the sky pinkened above, people started milling through town, heading off to their daily tasks. Many turned their heads in our direction.

"Come with me," he pleaded again, reaching for my hands.

I pulled away. "Will you save him?"

"I cannot. He is bound in iron behind an iron cage, underground. I dare not try."

"Then we have nothing more to discuss," I told him, continuing on my way.

He followed, but the gates drew close. I knew he would not pass under the cold leaden portcullis with me. His kind were highly averse, according to my mother's tales.

"Deirdre, I love you," he said, as if his heart were breaking.

That stopped me cold.

I turned.

His eyes flooded with tears.

I didn't know his kind could cry.

"Please, please don't leave me like this. Come with me, now, and I'll carry you away from here. You'll never know pain, fear, doubt, neglect, or self-hatred again. I will fill your cup with joy every day until the stars bleed from the heavens."

He was telling the truth.

I could feel it.

My hands shook. My collar grew damp.

But I did not go to him.

"Why didn't you tell me this years ago? Why tell me now?"

"I had hoped to, when you were ready to hear."

I heard him now. What was left of my heart shattered inside my chest like a physical wound. But still, I did not go to him.

I wanted to.

I *needed* to.

But I would not.

"Briar," I said, wiping my face with the back of my hand. "I might have loved you too, were I worthy of it."

Without another word, I turned on my heel, and resumed my march upward, toward the dour gray keep looming below the salmon-colored clouds ahead.

Twenty-One

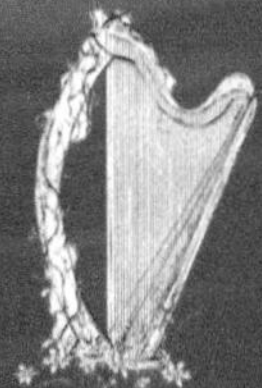

The morning of Breccan's execution dawned gray and cold as a pearl. An oppressive white fog curled through every lane like the searching fingers of an angry god. Townsfolk shuttered their windows as I passed, stuffing rags into the gaps to ward off the oncoming chill. Winter was near. Most knew better than to linger outdoors on such a day. Only a few stragglers and perverse voyeurs wished to stand outside in such miserably cold weather to watch a young man burn to death.

Many would catch a cough in the next few weeks that would soon become a fever. Several of them would be buried before Imbolc. I didn't need Briar's foresight for that. This was Ulaid, and people died in droves as soon as the first winter squall blew in from the west. It happened every year. Nor was I immune. Frigid damp air stung my cheeks and sought to steal my breath.

I drew my shawl tight but soldiered on.

I had somewhere to be, even if half the town would prefer to spare themselves.

Poor wage for an hour's entertainment.

Those who lived within the keep would certainly risk the elements today. The spectacle they sought would warm them plenty. I marched uphill with as much confidence as I could muster, both thankful for the general lack of spectators gathering in the lanes and equally horrified by the thought. Both Breccan and I were bound to die today, and no one but my own cursed family would be around to witness it. I struggled up the muddy street, fully conscious that I did so for the last time. Tears threatened to spill from my eyes, but I swiped them away lest they freeze against my skin.

I would not weep.

I would not bend.

What had my life been for, if not for this moment?

I expected my entrance to the square to be blocked by at least a few guards and fur-draped nobles, but I didn't see anyone until I was well within striking range of the pyre. Only a few people had gathered, myself included, beneath sodden awnings and dripping doorstops. The guards were sparse, and thus far, fewer than a dozen spectators had accumulated in the square to watch the day's bonfire.

And what a sight it was.

The wood must have come from the north, as it was a pale, fragrant pine that contrasted sharply with its dull gray surroundings. Such a sight was rare in Emain Macha. Too new, too bright to last. But of course, it would be aflame in under an hour. Taking my Breccan with it. All that beautiful wood hacked apart and hewn together to murder an innocent boy. As my boot scraped the large granite flagstones that marked the common square, the sun cut a sliver through the gloom, just as the keep's portcullis rattled upward. The nobles and their awful, tonsured priest came down to the square in a colorful line, each wearing more furs than half the townsfolk has ever owned. Faces I didn't recognize came first, some yawning, some scowling, one woman muttering about the unseemly hour. When the king's party came under the heavy iron gate, his new queen complained bitterly of the cold.

I steeled myself.

These horrible people.

They didn't even have the decency to assume a somber facade on such a terrible day. To them, it was just another day.

Just another commoner to be punished for their fear. Another innocent life sacrificed for their comfort, their peace of mind, their grip on power. I watched my cousin cradle his delicate new bride and frown at the sky. The queen shivered against him in her lush ermine cloak, her full lips pulled into a pale, bloodless pout. Well, at least they weren't comfortable.

That was something.

As for me, my fingers had long gone blue holding my shawl beneath my chin.

I was soaked through already, boots sopping and coated in mud. If I managed to survive the day, I was sure to develop a fever soon after. But I knew that wasn't going to happen.

Today I would win Breccan's freedom.

Today I would pay for my sins.

Calanthe, I thought silently.

Today, you have your reckoning.

We will be together soon.

WHEN THEY DRAGGED BRECCAN BENEATH THE PORTCUL-lis, I gasped to see how thin and gaunt he'd become. His copper hair hung in greasy tendrils over his brow and ears. The lovely tunic I'd made him hung from him in filthy rags, revealing glimpses of emaciated, bruised white skin. He blinked at the light, thin though it was, his long lashes brushing against the hollows of his eyes. He was weeping as they led him to the square.

My hand flew to my mouth.

A shabby shopkeeper beside me giggled as if I'd made a joke. "Ghastly sight, to be sure."

"Oh aye," said another onlooker. "Fairies look to have sucked his marrow clean."

Two guards stood on Breccan's either side, arms hooked firmly under his, half escorting, half dragging him along.

His eyes flared at the sight of the pyre. He blubbered, trying to backpedal. "No!" he sobbed. "No, *no, no!*"

Without mercy, the guards jerked him upright with force enough to snap his jaws together. I saw blood dribble down his chin, and knew he'd bitten his tongue. He wept openly, screwing his eyes shut tight. They dragged him up the steps, bodily. He kicked, flailed, and fought but it made no difference. He might have been a child throwing a tantrum. One guard pushed him against the post by his forehead, while the other tied his hands behind his back.

"Oh, now this should be fun," said the shopkeep.

I prayed for the patience not to murder the man on the spot.

I shifted forward.

It wouldn't be long now.

My cousin, the king, stepped forward while they lashed Breccan to the pine mast at the pyre's center. He looked bored.

"Today," he sighed, as if weary in his bones, "we set an example for all spirits and fairies tempted to enter this kingdom through its people. Those who would curse this land with ill luck and dark magic." He gestured to Breccan. "This lad carried these evils into the heart of my hall, at my own wedding feast."

Breccan moaned something, but the blood running down his face told me his tongue had swollen past the point of speech.

I took a step forward.

Then another.

The king looked around at his wedding guests, now witnesses to this execution. I understood that to his mind, after what had happened to my family, he felt he had no choice. If he cared in the least. It didn't matter.

I would stop this.

I took another step.

Then another.

One of the guards noticed me, head swiveling to watch me approach.

"Those who treat with The Others cannot be permitted to dwell in these lands," said the king.

The crowd muttered its agreement.

Someone yawned.

Breccan whimpered as I passed him, but I doubt he saw me. A second guard watched me approach and held a mailed arm out to bar me. I had made it past the pyre. Several pairs of eyes slid over me, appraising and dismissing.

The king raised a brow. "You would speak for the lad, woman?"

I dug deep inside myself, looking for something solid to give me strength.

Flashes of my life danced past my eyes at that moment.

Breccan at my hearthfire grinning over town gossip. Breccan in the river as a boy.

Cook teaching me how to divide a garden into fallow and fecund portions.

Cook and I in the wagon on the way north.

My father's face as he sat in my room the last time I saw him, tears in his eyes.

Calanthe.

Briar.

I saw everything.

I *felt* everything.

My eyes stung.

But I did not cower.

I stood up taller, shrugging my shall away so my cousin might get a good look at my green eyes. The barest flicker of recognition— or near that— crossed his face, which was so like mine.

"This boy is not fey-touched and has brooked no covenants with The Others," I declared, as loudly as possible.

The crowd murmured.

The guards got close.

But the king held out a hand.

"How do you know this?"

I heard Breccan muttering behind me and steeled myself once more. "If you search through his belongings, you will find a box bearing a golden braid."

"Aye," the queen's stout priest agreed. "We did find such. Had an unholy shine that fetish."

I nodded once. "As well it might, for it belonged to Calanthe Ap Muirdagh."

The murmur grew louder and more discordant.

"*Ap Muirdagh*?" asked the king, incredulously. "You mean to tell me this boy stole something from my own long dead cousin?"

"No, he stole it from *me*. Your long banished cousin, Deirdre." The crowd seemed to recoil and lean closer at the same time. The small priest crossed himself, while the king's brehon called to Brida for protection. I tossed my hair as I might have done in my youth, and pointed. "The lad has no contract with The Others, but *I* do."

"She will curse us!" cried the queen, flinching away from her husband to clutch at the priest's robes.

"Kill her!" someone else, probably the tall bald brehon with the blue whorls beneath his eyes.

But the guards hesitated, as I'd hoped they would.

No one wanted to share my family's curse.

Several of the gathered townsfolk screamed and fled from the square. I moved closer to Breccan, grabbing the dagger from my belt. "If you wish to break this curse, you burn the wrong witch."

With the nobles' eyes on me, I climbed up the pyre to Breccan's side. The priest seemed to remember himself, his piggish face puckering. "Kill them! Burn them both!"

I gave the little coward my best smile. "If you shed this innocent blood, I vow doom will visit this house for a hundred generations. I swear it on Macha's blood, which flows through these veins."

I didn't wait for his reply.

I moved behind Breccan, sawing into his bonds with my dagger. He choked and sputtered, pleading with only his eyes.

"Listen to me," I whispered into his ear, watching the nobles slowly recover from this incredible shock. I saw fire pass beneath the portcullis. Shouts rang around the guardhouse. The king seemed to blink himself awake. "When you are free, get down and run. Don't turn around and don't ever come back here. Do you hear me?"

Great, fat tears rolled down his bloodied, hollow cheeks. He bobbed his head, but moaned something I took to mean 'come with me.' I was more afraid than I'd ever been in my whole life. But I didn't let him see. Once his hands were free, I cupped his chin and kissed his brow. "Go, *now!*"

Reluctantly, he obeyed me.

I watched him tumble down the pyre and push past the guards, who stood dumbfounded nearby. He turned to look back at me just as the first torch struck the timbers beneath my feet. Flames leaping to life behind me, I smiled and waved goodbye. Dark clouds spooled above.

A wicked wind fed the fire.

I felt its heat kiss my heels.

Breccan's harp was tossed onto the pyre beneath me.

I could swear I heard Calanthe sigh.

I clutched at the mast at the center, where Breccan had been tied, searching for any scrap of courage I could muster.

I had so many regrets.

So many things I had never done.

So many things I had never said.

"Briar," I pleaded with the wind as it licked flames into my hem. "I did love you. Forgive me."

"Deirdre Ap Muirdagh," bellowed my cousin, the king. "You are condemned to die for the sins of kinslaying and darkcraft. Die honorably, and take your curses with you!"

His queen howled agreement.

The crowd moved back, aghast but expectant.

Any witch was better than none.

The flames reached the flesh at my foot. The pain was exquisite. I wailed as my skin melted away and the fats in my foot began to pop and hiss. My dress caught next, and I screamed until my throat pinched off. I collapsed against the mast, holding on for dear life. The flames licked up my thighs and I couldn't scream anymore. White hot spears of pain raced through my heart until it beat futilely against my ribs, a trapped rabbit in a burning cage. The smoke soon struck my face, blocking my throat, and I could feel or see nothing. All was pain. All was anguish.

Then, through that din, I heard the clean, clear chime of a tiny bronze bell. A single, pure note piercing the fog in my mind.

Cool, strong hands reached out to cover mine.

A presence I knew as well as my own shadow blocked the flames as it came to stand behind me. "Deirdre," Briar said, his lips at my ear, the pain fading into the shelter of his body. "Will you come with me now?"

Distantly, I could hear the crackling flames and the vitriol spouted by the onlookers.

"I… I'm afraid."

"Courage like yours need never fear again."

I turned in his arms.

His bright green eyes smiled down into mine.

Above him, the sky raced west, chasing the dark clouds away.

The air filled with sunlight and birdsong.

The flames had gone.

In their place, soft velvet and silk skirts pooled around my slippered feet. Such finery, I'd never seen before— and I, the daughter of a king. Gold rings bedecked my fingers, and my long dark hair was swept high above my collar, peppered with gems. Around my neck, a tiny golden bell swung from a delicate gold chain. Briar brought my unmarred fingers to his full lips, and I clung to him. In the distance behind us, I caught a glimpse of a high tower gleaming against a star-washed, lavender sky.

He took my hand to lead me away.

And I knew I was finally safe.

Finally free.

"Let's go home," he said.

And home, I went.

Other Works by LM Riviere

The Innisfail Cycle Series

The Sons of Mil

The Southernmost Star

The Children of Danu

Coming Soon

A Vow for Breaking (2026)

A Devil for Delilah Winter (2026)